KINDERLAND

KINDERLAND

a novel

LILIANA COROBCA

TRANSLATED BY **MONICA CURE**

SEVEN STORIES PRESS
NEW YORK · OAKLAND

Support for this publication has been provided by a grant
from the Romanian Cultural Institute's Translation and
Publication Support program

 INSTITUTUL
CULTURAL
R O M Â N

Seven Stories Press
140 Watts Street
New York, NY 10013
www.sevenstories.com

College professors and high school and middle school teachers may order free examination
copies of Seven Stories Press titles. Visit https://www.sevenstories.com/pg/resources-academics
or email academic@sevenstories.com.

Library of Congress Cataloging-in-Publication Data

Names: Corobca, Liliana, author. | Cure, Monica, translator.
Title: Kinderland : a novel / Liliana Corobca ; translated by Monica Cure.
Other titles: Kinderland. English
Description: New York : Seven Stories Press, [2023]
Identifiers: LCCN 2023023349 | ISBN 9781644213278 (trade paperback) | ISBN
  9781644213285 (ebook)
Subjects: LCGFT: Domestic fiction.
Classification: LCC PC840.413.O763 K5613 2023 | DDC
  859/.335--dc23/eng/20230524
LC record available at https://lccn.loc.gov/2023023349

Printed in the USA

9 8 7 6 5 4 3 2 1

The tick was stuck to his stomach, next to his belly button, sucking the child's blood. The girl, more terrified by her brother's shrieks than by that black dot, had gone for help. Normally, the howls would have brought out, if not half the village, at least the entire neighborhood on the outskirts of the village, but now, no one came. She could've taken out the tick, but what if the head got stuck there and it grew another body that was even bigger . . . or, God forbid, it went completely inside his skin and lodged there, where no one could get it out anymore and her brother would die, sucked dry by the tick.

At first, the third child, the youngest brother, who was often hit or mistreated by the other one, looked on with a certain sense of satisfaction. He kept circling his older brother in search of what was making him cry and yell so insistently. He looked around, up, down, to see whether he didn't also have cause to let out a wail, but he didn't see anything. The fact that Dan's shirt was lifted, his belly naked and exposed to the sun, didn't impress the younger brother at all, it didn't scare him either. The black dot his brother was hunched over so tragically didn't interest him since he couldn't understand how a brother so big and strong could be scared by a little black dot clinging to his belly. Then the younger little boy disappeared.

The girl went out on the street. She could've called the neighbors, but they weren't home at this hour. The grandmother of a classmate lived farther down, but she probably wasn't home either and, in any case, her eyesight wasn't good enough to get the tick out, head and all. The girl started walking down the street, in search of the right person. She also called out to Uncle Vasile, but all the dogs in the neighborhood answered her instead. At the barking of the dogs in unison, nothing happened inside the houses, no one slammed the doors or gates, no one opened them to see who was calling and why. In general, when someone called out on their street, they all heard and at least someone would answer: The person you're looking for isn't home, they've just left for the vineyard, to visit their godfather, or somewhere else. At the end of the street, she spotted a mother washing clothes in a courtyard. She didn't know her name. She made noise as she opened the gate and the woman looked at her questioningly.

— Hello. Would you mind taking out a tick for us?

The woman wrinkled her nose in disgust and answered:

— I don't take out ticks.

And the woman quickly went inside the house.

The girl stopped next to the well. Maybe someone would get thirsty and come by for some water. She would stay there and wait.

Meanwhile, the youngest brother brought the other brother his favorite toy. The brother with the tick ignored him. He couldn't care less about toys right now.

It seemed like Dan would never stop crying. In the past, he had killed insects like that, which his dad had taken out of the sheep's wool. His father had said that if you don't take them out, ticks suck all the blood out of an animal until there's nothing left of it. Dan imagined how the hungry tick would suck up all his blood until it became a kind of big balloon and he, small and withered, a bag of bones, would helplessly flutter his arms and legs, while the tick would start floating until it was high up in the sky. Hundreds of ticks, inflated with the blood of children, floated in the clear, smiling sky, while the scrawny, dried-out kids stuck to the ruthless bugs cried. Dan looked at his tick which, to be honest, was no bigger than half a pinky fingernail, in fact, it wasn't even as big as a bean, but all the same he felt as if he didn't have a drop of blood left in him.

Marcel had remembered about the beautiful apple, which he had found the day before yesterday and hidden so that he could eat it by himself, without sharing with his brother and sister. The neighbor's apple tree had produced fruit this year and sometimes an apple would fall into their garden. Summer apples, sweet and with pink flesh. Dan, when he saw the apple, made a gesture as if to say: What's your apple to me when I'm in pain! Then Marcel, out of brotherly solidarity, started to whimper as well.

A horse-drawn cart stopped next to the well. A man drew out a bucket of water, drank some, and then wet his horse's nose. He looked back at the girl staring at him. Tall, skinny, ugly, almost toothless, thin and graying hair, big floppy ears, he could've played the part of the grim reaper if he had kept a scythe in his cart. The horse was also skinny, it had once been gray but now, dirty, it was an earthy greenish color, with long yellow teeth, as if to make up for its master.

— Would you mind taking out a tick?
— Not at all. Where is it?

— There, said Cristina as she pointed toward the gate.

— Whose daughter are you?

— My dad's Victor Dumitrache.

— Well, well, you're Vichiuşa's daughter? I used to give you cart rides when you were little. Back then I had a strong, sleek stallion . . . And your pa's gone off to make long money. The girl nodded. And he left you at the mercy of the ticks. The girl nodded again.

When they saw the man come in, the two brothers went silent, forgetting to cry.

— Where are you, tick?

Then he looked at the apple.

— What, you don't want your apple? Let's give it to the pony, he'll gobble it right up!

The smaller boy again handed the apple to the bigger one, who, given the choice between him or the horse eating it, decided to take the apple without saying a word. When it came down to it, the man was scarier to him than the tick.

— What, you call that a tick, boy, it's as small as an ant! Lemme at it!

Then he said to the girl:

— Do you have brandy or odikolon?

She did, and she went to get the alcohol. She thought to herself: He wants to drink it, get drunk, and toss my brothers over the fence.

The man approached the afflicted child. He fiercely gritted his few teeth at the tick, a gesture which made the littlest one run behind the house. He poked his head out from behind a corner after a moment because he didn't hear anything and he was curious.

In the blink of an eye, the man squeezed the swollen tick

between his blackened fingernails and threw it onto the ground, looking carefully at the boy's belly.

— I got it out, head and all, he said with satisfaction. Now step on it.

Because the boy didn't move, he called over the little one:

— Hey, come here, little snot-nose, come look at your brother's tick. But the little one didn't accept the invitation either. The girl approached with a small bottle, out of which the man poured some brandy into his palm and then rubbed it onto the boy's belly.

— Okay, you step on it, he said to the girl.

The girl conscientiously put her foot down on the bug and jumped on it a few times.

— And you say your pa's not home.

The children nodded their heads.

— So he's off working. Three kids are no laughing matter. And your ma—she's working too. They had you and then scattered every which way, said the man as he headed to the gate. My woman's gone too, so are my kids. I'm all by my lonesome, lucky I got my horse. Come on, filly, let's go home.

The noise of the wheels could be heard for a little while, and then silence.

The girl, too, poured a little bit of alcohol from the bottle into her palm and rubbed the belly of the child, who was sitting gravely, without moving a muscle, looking somewhere off into the distance. Of course, if Dad had been home, no tick would've stuck to him, it wouldn't have gone under his skin. He felt a kind of dissatisfaction that everything had ended so simply and quickly, when he had had an excuse to be unhappy, coddled, and important.

———

There were so few kids on their street that you couldn't put caterpillars in anyone's hair, or beetles down anyone's shirt, you couldn't blow up a decent frog with anyone. Dan had already become bored with his little brother, who wasn't afraid of caterpillars or beetles anymore. If he stuffed one in his shirt, Marcel laughed like an idiot, because his brother was playing with him and giving him attention. He couldn't play with his older sister either, except when she wanted, and how she wanted, and if something wasn't to her liking, she could make you behave immediately with a punch in the back or a kick in the butt. Also, his older sister had chased off all the boys Dan played with. Now he would no longer tell her who beat him up, because he risked not having anyone left to play with. The boys avoided him thanks to the memory of the pinching and hair-pulling they got after a run-in with his scrappy sister. Even Dan was amazed. How could Cristina, as scrawny and tiny as she was, just skin and bones, you'd have thought the wind would blow her away, put to flight a bunch of good-for-nothings who were that big, fat, and strong, who had their mothers and fathers at home? One time he, too, saw her and got scared. The girl had gotten a running start, her hair stood on end, she stretched out her claws toward the enemy, as if possessed by all the animals in the world, then she screamed so shrilly that her voice could break your eardrum, and the speed at which she rushed the unprepared enemy, no matter how big or powerful he might be, made him take off.

Cristina now has a small mark, a scar on her cheek. From a prideful boy she had turned into a laughingstock. She had seen him beat up Dan, her beloved brother, whom no one besides her could protect. She stalked the boy one rainy day when he was coming home from school, all nicely dressed in his blue shirt, along with two classmates, a girl and a boy. Cristina waited next to a big puddle and, when the three walked by her, she pushed the bully in, which made the other two burst into laughter. He decided he'd smash her head in at the first chance he got, he'd teach her, puny, ugly girl, to throw him into the mud. When the moment came, he bombarded her with rocks until her face was all bloody, then he got scared and ran away. Cristina was glad, judging from the size of his pile of rocks, she wouldn't have made it home in one piece if he hadn't stopped. And who would take care of her brothers? This way, she got off with just a busted up cheek—he could've hit her in the eyes, or cracked her head open. A cheek would go back into place. She put a wet hand towel on her face and thought up her next plan for revenge.

The boy didn't live too far from their house, he didn't have an older brother, or a dad, not even one who had gone after long money, and his mom was away in the city, looking for work. He lived for the most part with a mean grandmother, who put him to work and beat him from time to time, so he wouldn't get spoiled. She wasn't sure what his name was, maybe Aurel. He was a grade older.

Supposedly, back in the day when their mom was in school, there were two classes in each grade, class A and class B, and during the time of their grandparents, they even had a class C. There were so many kids back then! Now it's hard to make up one class from three or four villages. The teachers come by people's gates to ask kids to come to school. Before, the village was split in half: one half was class A, the other B. The kids learned how to put on gas masks, to shoot firearms, they searched out wooden grenades hidden in the forest, they organized military school competitions. The girls also shot firearms—if they were too weak or too short, they'd lie down on their bellies and aim. They were put into first aid teams. You had to give medical attention to the sick, to know what medicinal plants were good for, to carry the wounded if they had a broken bone, to give mouth-to-mouth to someone who had fainted. Cristina learned a little bit from her mother and grandmother, so she could help her brothers if anything ever happened. One summer, when she started watering the cucumbers, she tripped on a thick rusty wire which pierced her skin. It hurt so badly that she forgot to wash the wound and the amount of blood spilling out scared her. But she quickly found a big fleawort leaf, wiped it with the back of her hand (it was clean anyway), and applied it to the wound. The leaf stuck to her leg and Cristina went on watering the cucumbers. When she remembered about the gash, the leaf was very dry, like hay in the winter, and the wound was just a line, that's all. As if nothing had happened. Her mother used to say: Quickly, everything's done quickly. Bandage it quickly. Wash it quickly, when you've stained your clothes or a tablecloth. If you wash the stain quickly, it comes out easily, without too much effort . . .

For a while now, Aurel had been playing cards right next to their walnut tree on the other side of the fence, with two other boys. Cristina watched him a few times and got an idea for the worst punishment she could inflict, in revenge for her busted up cheek. While he sat under the walnut tree, she, from the other side of the fence, would slowly dump a cow pie, soft and smelly, right on his head. Cows passed by on the street twice a day and each dropped a big cow pie. She'd shovel one up and stick it under the fence. Besides the fact that the smell could kill you, cow pies had this intense green color, which you couldn't get out with anything. So it would ruin his clothes too. She could already feel herself triumphant and avenged. She imagined the scene. In her mind she watched her pathetic enemy crying and running to his grandma who couldn't do anything about it. Finding a cow pie wasn't a problem, but she had to make sure it didn't dry out, so it would be soft and ooze down his face, ears, neck, under the collar of his shirt. Every Thursday and Friday, the boys definitely would come around three or four and leave in the evening when it got dark. Pushing it with a hoe, Cristina got a cow pie onto a shovel and left it by the fence. The kids, who didn't even suspect the pungent and threatening presence of the cow pie (though it smelled horrific), sat down by the fence, right next to the spot where the loaded up shovel waited on the other side, so all Cristina had to do was to aim at Aurel, avoiding the other, innocent, children, and dump it straight on his head. The girl hid behind the fence and listened in on the children's conversation. The three boys had started playing cards, cussing like a bunch of grown men. Then they talked admiringly about a classmate of theirs who had found some dried tobacco (put between layers of folded clothes to guard against moths). He had rolled it in grape leaves and taken a few puffs. But like that's smoking—that's for babies! There are boys in their class who smoke real cigarettes in the restroom, expensive ones, the kind the other boys drool over. Cristina got tired of listening to them, she lifted the shovel and leaned against the fence, over Aurel's head. She paused for a second with her shovel in the air, then she changed her mind. When the enemy is helpless and defenseless, she forgives, she doesn't strike . . . She's much more powerful if she forgives him. Quite pleased with herself and proud that she was a girl who was so upright and generous, she took the shovel and dumped it out underneath a tree in the garden, so that it would produce better fruit thanks to the natural fertilizer. Then she went out on the street with a bucket to get some water from the well. The boys paid no attention to her. They had no clue what an unpleasant surprise had been waiting for them just a few moments ago.

∾

Dear parents!
　The days pass so slowly without you! Today is Sunday.
　I know what we'll do today. We'll go on a trip to the other end of the village, to see Kamchatka. That's what Ghiță's house is called now ever since his pa brought him two new brothers, two wild children from far-off Russia. They're dark, stocky, and short, though the older one is almost seven years old and he'll have to start going to school. They babble to each other and no one can understand them. They have narrow, slanted eyes, like bigger button loops on a sheepskin coat or a puffy winter jacket and, for this reason, the older one is nicknamed Buttonloop. The younger one is called Puppydog, because he's always under the table and he crawls around on all fours more than walks, and whimpers more than speaks. We don't know how old Puppydog is, maybe three years old, maybe four.
　Ghiță says they aren't his brothers. They embarrass him and he kind of hits them. The villagers go to see them as if they were going to a circus, and they stay hidden under the table, only peeking their heads out, like a couple of scared ani-

mals. They stay under there all day, even if Ghiță sometimes pokes them with a broom to come out. People throw them bread, apples, and walnuts under the table, and they munch on them. We don't come empty-handed either—I bought a pack of cookies and Dan gave it to the younger one. Marcel goes under the table as well and they play there. They have an entire setup under the table, with a long thick sheepskin, a little chair they use as a table, and lots of toys, both real and makeshift. The tablecloth is so long it reaches all the way down to the carpet, and covers everything under the table. The kids know how to say their names, and when they laugh, you can see their dimples. I immediately forget their names after a few seconds. They're impossible to remember. Dan is the same age as Buttonloop and he got the idea to get him out from under the table and for them to learn to write together. The other boy came out for a little bit, but he didn't like writing so he went back under the table.

Ghiță wasn't home, we would've talked about school because we're in the same class. I felt lonely. I would've gone under the table too, but there was no more room. When we were leaving, Marcel didn't want to come out from under there anymore, that's how much he liked it. Dan dragged him out. I'm afraid to leave my brothers for too long with these kids. What if they've got some disease . . . If they've brought over some virus from that Kamchatka of theirs? They sit under the table all the time, when do they wash themselves? Ghiță said that their type of body requires them to wash themselves only once every season. They say that their dad had them with a dumb young Asian woman from Siberia, I think she wasn't that pretty, judging from the looks of these two. His grandma said that they're not her son's, that the Asian woman had already had them.

Ghiţǎ's mom is always off somewhere, but that started not too long ago, because her husband had been sending money and she stayed home, like a grand lady. Then less and less money started coming in. Meaning it was being shared with someone, that's a sure sign, everyone knows. But to go so far as to bring foreign kids into your home, to make your entire family a laughingstock . . .

I'm going to ask Dad to keep his Eskimos, Chuvans, Karelians, Portuguese, and other button loop people there with him, if he has any, and not embarrass us. Our mom left home too because Dad didn't bring in enough money. Now Ghiţǎ's mom sells walnuts in the city, it's the most profitable thing, walnuts are expensive and they don't go bad overnight. In any case, for now she has money, she asked her husband for some because of the kids he brought in. She told him that if he doesn't give her money, she'll take them into the forest and leave them there to be eaten by wolves. Because she started having nightmares every night since the moment she laid eyes on them. She was already tired of raising their own children by herself, then the cheating sonafabitch brings her a cartful of savage button loop brats that hide under the table all day. It was such a scandal at first . . . People go off to make money often enough, every family has someone working abroad, sometimes men cheat because, duh, they're far away from their wives and they have their urges and needs, but they're not quick to have more children, after you can barely provide for the ones you have back home. Well, if it happened to turn out that way, what can you do, at least keep them there, deep in Siberia, the woman who gave birth to them can take care of them. Have only a few villagers added to the population of the places they went to? Tons must have screwed up . . . But no, he brings them home to me, to make me the butt of jokes, so the entire village knows . . . And not one, but two. And not even with a beautiful, plump Russian woman, but with an Asian woman or whatever she is, and he brings me these bowlegged, filthy, stuttering, mangy dogs, so ugly they'll give you nightmares! But actually, they're not that ugly, they've got dimples when they laugh. Apparently, their fight was so big that they almost beat each other up. Ghiță's dad is a softie, that's why all the women take advantage of him. He promised his wife that he wouldn't have any other children with the Asian woman. And he'll take them back as soon as he can. And it's not her who's taking care of them, but their grandma, meaning his mother. And he leaves them money enough. Ghiță's mom, steaming mad, left for the city.

✁

When Dan was young, he was such a spoiled little liar! Our parents were home and I didn't hit him, I only threatened him, all I did was lower my eyebrows a bit into a frown and he'd start wailing immediately. More like screaming, actually, at the top of his lungs, so that Mom would rush in to see what had happened and he'd say: She punched me in the stomach, or she punched me in the head. Mom would get furious and she'd ask me: Why would you hit him, punch him even, can't you see he's a little child? I tried to explain that I didn't even touch him . . . Mom: Then why is he screaming like that?

The more Mom scolded me, the happier Dan was. Well, I'll show you! I'd wait for Mom to leave and give Dan a kick straight in the butt. And this time, he wouldn't even cry because Mom couldn't hear him. He'd run away and hide.

Once, he broke a mug and hid it under the table. He waited for Mom to sweep it up and he yelled, pointing his finger at me:

Tina, Tina! Meaning me, Cristina. He was as small and chubby as a donut, he'd roll around more than walk. Mom didn't believe him. But he waited for Mom to scold me or hit me. Mom called me over, though she knew it wasn't me but him who did the deed, and she pretended to scold me to see what Dan would do. Dan imitated Mom who was shaking her finger, pretending to say, how could you, you broke the mug. I said:

What mug, it wasn't me!

Then Mom:

Maybe it was you, Dan?

No, Tina, Tina.

Let's ask the mug. Little mug, who broke you?

And I whispered quietly:

Daaan!

See, the mug says you broke it.

And when Dan started crying, I couldn't get him to calm down. I think he got scared because the mug told the truth, not because he was ashamed of being a liar!

When I was little, I didn't have brothers or sisters. I still don't have any sisters. Instead of two brothers, I would've liked to have had a brother and a sister. But two brothers is good too. Marcel can be a sister sometimes. Dan doesn't want to. Mom kept some nicer dresses of mine and when I'd try to dress up Dan in one of them, he'd yell loud enough to wake up the whole neighborhood. And when I'd call him Dana, he'd get mad. 'Cause he's a man, his name is Dan. Marcie sounds like a cow's name and I don't like calling Marcel that. I don't know why Mom and Dad would name my little brother something like that. They could've asked me. He doesn't cry when I put dresses or bows on him. I ask him if he wants to be a girl for a little bit, he sits there calmly and behaves himself, I take him to the mirror and put little bows in his hair, I like playing with his ringlets. I make sure not to pull on his hair so he doesn't cry. When Dan comes, he ruins everything. He laughs at Marcel, pinches him, calls him Marcie-Daisy, Marcie-Fartsy, mommy's little girl, until Marcel bursts into tears and doesn't want to wear a dress anymore. Dan says to him: You're a man! What man wears a dress!

Marcel plays with dolls too. He took one of mine, a little one, and made a bed for her, he has a handkerchief he covers her with. When I found her and asked him why he took my doll, he said it's not a doll, it's a biker, but he's little and he has to grow some more. I didn't tell Dan, who makes guns out of sticks all day, he scribbles on them with crayons and he shoots us from behind corners. When the two of them play, Dan always shoots Marcel, who has to stay shot down for as long as Dan wants. Marcel has already learned how to die believably, like in movies, to fall suddenly, as if gunned down, to Dan's great delight. Sometimes I go looking for Marcel, but I don't see him, I don't hear him. I hope nothing's happened to him. I find him under a tree. Dan shot him and forgot about him and Marcel is lying dead under the tree waiting to be ordered to come back to life. He's waiting for Dan to come get him. If I call him, he doesn't want to come, because he's waiting for Dan. If I say to him, hey dummy, Dan forgot about you, he's out on the street playing with some other boys, Marcel gets very upset, he even cries, 'cause why did Dan leave him shot under the tree.

Mom only wanted two children. Dad wanted Marcel. She said: We barely have food enough for these two. Dad said, let there be another kid, I'll go to Yakutiya, to work and make some money, and we'll have enough for the kids! We have lots of relatives and neighbors in Yakutiya, in Italy too. But in the beginning Dad didn't send any money, because he didn't make much and he had to pay back debts. Then a relative in Italy said to Mom: Come over here, a spot has opened up with a family, they pay well; if you don't want to come, a hundred Moldovans would kill to get here . . . Mom talked it over with Dad, then with me, and she said she'd go for a year or two, until Dad pays off his debts. Then she left, and that year or two never seems to end. Mom wants to find Dad work in Italy too, though Dad likes it in Russia. She dreams of the two of them saving enough money for a house in Italy and bringing us all over there, and making us Italians. *Grazie, signore!* But it's pretty hard to find jobs for men, so we'll be home alone for a while yet. She said it's nice in Italy, warm, pretty, almost like in Moldova, except that we wouldn't have apricot trees in our yard, nor plum trees. I think it's best in Moldova.

⁕

One's crying, the other wants food and turns everything upside down in the kitchen looking for sugar. I gave them jam, but they say all that jam and bread hurts their stomach. I saw someone, poorer than us, take slices of bread, wet them under the faucet, and dip them in sugar. From then on, the kids only wanted to eat bread with sugar and they stick soggy bread into the bag of sugar and get it wet, and it makes me mad. It's enough for the older one to cry for who knows what reason, for the little one to start wailing too, as if on cue. And they both cry tirelessly, for a long time, like a couple of wolf pups abandoned in the forest. They want someone to coddle them, to pay attention to them. I do too, even if I'm big. I also want a mother here with me, to make me something to eat, to wash my dresses. And to iron them.

I said to them, hold up your heart with just the tips of your fingers and blow on it hard, until it flies away to Mom. And then she'll cuddle those tubby kids who grow up eating mangos as if she were cuddling us. Isn't it true that you cry too when you think about us? And when you wash their little clothes, made from real wool, cotton, pure silk, made by silk worms, you think about our clothes, most of which are theirs, after the Italians have worn them and they've gotten old, they give them to you, so you can take them to us. If my brothers knew, they wouldn't even wear them anymore. It would be better not to have so many brand-name, natural fiber clothes, but have our mother instead. Maybe those kids, too, are well-behaved and sweet, and they also cry because their mother has left them to be cared for by a foreign woman.

Night and day you're with foreign kids, Mom, you take them for walks, play with them, feed them, tell them bedtime stories. And no one stays with us, we eat whatever we can, bread with sugar or smoked sausages from the store. And no one sings to us at night, at bedtime. I'd sing, but I don't know any songs. Dan learned a song in kindergarten about a foolish rabbit and he sings it so sadly, it's as if his entire family died and he's at their funeral right now. You stay there and make money. You send us some so we can have food to eat, supposedly. But nothing we buy from the store is good. Even the cat, no matter how hungry it might be, won't touch the store-bought food. Because they bring all kinds of trash into our poor and unhappy country, all those chemicals, things that are rotten, expired drumsticks that don't go bad even if you leave them out in the sun for a week, sour cream you can paint your fence with and then lick a month later, it has the same taste, juice that cleans rust off of sinks. Mothers make their children chicken soup, from the chickens in their yards, not the ones from the store that don't taste like anything.

What do kids there eat? Avocado spread on baguettes, with pink fish on top? Veal schnitzel with couscous and mangos and exotic herbs? When you come home, bring a mango for us too. I heard they're good, but I haven't tasted one yet. They say that anyway they can't be better than our juicy fragrant pears, that melt in your mouth . . .

Mom, is it true that there, where you are, kids are taken outside like dogs, on a leash, tied with little cords or straps? And that they're walked in groups of three or four or more? One day I tied up my two brothers, let's go take a walk, I said, the way they do in Europe. They only went a little ways, then they took off their reins: We're not colts. The whole village will laugh at us. Actually, an old baba came out of her yard and went:

— Pfft, you kooks! Why did you tie up the younguns? Why dontcha let them walk down the street like normal people?

And when I told her that's what they did in Europe and America, she said:

— Child, let the younguns go free, 'cause they'll tie themselves up enough as they grow up, and life will tie them up enough 'til old age.

Mom, if a kid falls down, it's easier to pick him up if he's tied to something, you don't have to bend over anymore. I think nannies tie them up for the sake of what's convenient for themselves, not the kids. If someone were to ask the kids, not one of them would say: Yes, I like being tied up. We have it better, us kids left home alone, no one ties us up or puts a harness on us, there's no one around to do it.

⁂

Several people from our village now have goats with long curved horns, the kind in cowboy movies. I don't know if their entire line comes from our goats, which seem to be mountain goats, judging by their horns. When our parents left, they gave our goats to some relatives, so we wouldn't have to deal with them. Meaning so I wouldn't have to deal with them, because as it is, I already have to look after two brothers, a dog, a cat, a pig, ten chickens, a scrappy rooster, the last thing I needed with this entire army was a bunch of goats. We sometimes get milk or cheese from our kinder relatives or the ones who at least have common decency, they give us something from our goats every now and then.

Auntie Vera went to a wedding with Uncle and she left me in charge of their farm, since their kids are younger, she doesn't trust them. So I had to take care of all their animals and their two coddled children, our cousins, and in the evening, I had to milk a goat. Their daughter said she was afraid of the goat, because it bites and pokes you with its horns. No one taught her how to milk animals. She acts like a little kid though I'm only two years older than her. She's sturdier and fatter, because her parents take good care of her, and she looks older than me.

To milk a goat, a stubborn animal, you need four kids to hold it, plus one to milk it. I told Lia that if she tells everyone that the animal bites, we won't find enough kids in the whole village to help us milk it. One already asked why Lia doesn't hold it, because it's her goat. Lia had thought of what to say and she told him: I hold its tail, because it's long and gets in the way of milking. The goat swishes its tail and Cristina (meaning me) can't milk it. She went on that in any case, she's a young lady and she isn't strong enough to hold onto its hoof. (Listen to that, a young lady!) Plus, someone has to hold onto its horns too so it doesn't poke us.

Lia came up with the idea to put a scarf over its head, including its muzzle, or to put a bag over it. Get outta here, you want to kill it or what! So your mom will beat me for suffocating her animal. Such a little goat. I'd rather not milk it. I found three kids, but all scaredy-cats. Only me and Dan aren't afraid of goats, the others had a cow or a horse at home and they looked at the goat as if it were a crocodile. A puny little boy, when I told him, hey, grab on here, got scared and started to cry. The ruckus also scared the goat and stopped up its milk.

I wasn't strong enough to pull harder on its teat and get the milk back down. It wouldn't have helped to be alone, without noisy kids, though, because when you're milking, it tickles the goat and it won't stay still, it runs away or pokes you, or it kicks its hoof and knocks over the container of milk, or even worse, it poops right into the container. The kids approached the goat as if it were an ogre. Each of them grabbed onto a leg while threatening it. The goat didn't move, it was stock-still, we couldn't tell if it was even breathing. From time to time it tried to let out a desperate bleat which sounded really weird because it had a pail on its head, to keep it from biting us. That had been our solution, to let it breathe but not bite us. Poor thing, maybe it had never bitten anyone in its whole life. There was no more room next to the goat, I couldn't reach the teat with everyone crowded around. The goat allowed me to milk it, more or less. The kids, feeling victorious, started to relax, and then the goat seized the moment and thrashed violently, without managing to free itself. But it upset the pail with its three trickles of milk and I lost my balance, falling on my butt in the poop around there and getting my dress and hands dirty. The kids were dying of laughter, of course. You can't get animal poop out with anything, it's over, you've ruined your clothes and your very soul stinks of it. There's a reason why people who keep animals stink, you can tell by the smell which animals they have: sheep, cows, pigs, horses, goats. They get so used to the smell that they can't even tell it's there anymore, while it's enough to make other people's noses fall off. I was so mad I punched the pail . . .

— It'll hurt it if we don't milk it. All the milk's stuck in its teat.

— Let's bring it a baby goat, because there's no way we can milk it.

— It's not going to let an animal it doesn't know get close, can't you see it's wild?

— A yearling used to suck its milk, it would do that to all the sheep that didn't have lambs anymore and to this goat, after they butchered its baby. I don't know how they all let it. They sold the yearling last week.

They brought the goat two baby goats from the neighbor's, the baby goats were so fat that the kids could barely haul them. But the goat head-butted them away, they weren't in a hurry to drink its milk either, either they were already full or were scared by the unfamiliar place and so many onlookers.

After I wiped myself off with some hay, I tried milking it again. This time without a container, fine, let the milk spill on the floor. I pulled on its leg, I grabbed a teat, a trickle of milk came out. I pulled for a bit more, but I quickly got tired. Then the kids brought the container and I aimed the milk into it for a bit.

— Take this milk to the dog, he should feel like it's a holiday every once in a while.

Then the boys left to go play and we girls stayed to chat about homemaking, fashion, and men.

Grandma used to tell us stories, now we tell them to her. Every time she sees me, she asks:

— Whose are you?

I tell her each time, and she says: . . . Ahhh, little Vic, ah, the poor boy, he's slaving away (Grandma says: *slavin'*) among strangers, he can't eat his own bread at home . . . and you don't know when your pa's coming back . . . your ma's not there either . . .

I wouldn't be surprised to see her playing with Marcelly, she's become completely childish. Now Auntie Eudochia makes food for her. She says Grandma cries when she has to wash herself. And it smells bad at her place, as if she pees in her bed. Maybe she really does. She's changed so much! I don't want to criticize her too harshly, because she was a good grandma, she'd tell us stories and bake us Easter bread with crosses on it. Auntie says Grandma won't die until she sees all her children, to say goodbye to them.

I picked some apricots, the ripest ones, because she only likes ripe ones, when they're sweet and soft, and we went to visit her, as you told us to. She was sitting quietly in a corner next to a window, tiny, hunched over, bundled up, though it wasn't cold, and listening carefully. When I spoke to her, she began telling me everything that she had heard. She can't go outside anymore and she doesn't see that well, but she hears everything. She knows how many roosters she still has and how many hens, she has only one turkey left. She knows who's buying wine from the neighbors, who's walking past her gate, whose house a car parked at, who's talking to who. Grandma's eyes are bluest-blue and very gentle.

It's better that I don't tell anyone that my mom and dad aren't home, because all kinds of bad kids will come over, they'll steal your toys and eat the food off your table and even punch you in the back of the neck, if you put up a fight. And you have to be in good with everyone, to get along with them so that they don't steal something of yours, or beat you up, so that they have common decency . . . Mom, when you come home, I won't talk to anyone for three days. The next three days, I'll smack them all over the nose, those snots who beat up Dan and Marcel. I can't now, because they'd take revenge on my brothers, but when you come home, I'll catch them one by one and beat them to a pulp. That'll teach them not to pick on kids without parents! When you come, I'll be the proudest girl in the village. I'll wear that beautiful dress you brought me and twirl in it down the street like a turkey. It's prettier to twirl like a little peacock, that's what they call pretty girls, but I don't know how peacocks twirl.

Our house has become a shelter for kids whose parents beat them. Everyone knows we're home alone, because we're almost never visited by an old person, I mean an adult. If only the kids came full, not hungry, because they eat up all our food. They have mothers and fathers, sometimes just mothers, sometimes just fathers, but no one feeds them, they come dying of hunger and scarf down even plain bread as if real black caviar, fine and expensive, were spread on it, the kind we ate once when Mom came back from making long money.

   Whenever one comes by who has been beat up especially badly, I call over my brothers to listen. The kid answers all my questions. I ask him in detail on purpose:

— Did your dad punch you right in the head? Twice? So that it made you dizzy . . . Did blood drip from your nose too? A lot. Then did he also give you a kick in the butt? And he was drunk. He reeked and he went to the back of the garden to hurl, meaning to throw up everything in his alcohol-filled guts.

Then I give Marcel a meaningful look (the way Mom used to), Dan is big and already understands.

— Do you see, dummy, what a dad does? And you're wailing night and day. You want a dad so you can walk around with your head busted up, a bloody nose, hungry and in rags, and hide out at neighbors' houses? See how all the kids come to us because you're better off without a dad. We eat all kinds of treats from the store, everything our hearts desire, we've got enough money, we have toys and, since we've got things to play with, all the kids come over, because they don't and they want to steal one of ours, or just break one, out of spite.

Marcel, pouty and stubborn, doesn't say anything. He wants to answer back, but doesn't know what to say. He can't think of a single example of a good dad, who stays at home with his kids and takes care of them, loves them, the way he imagines. Everyone who comes to our house complains. Maybe there are good dads too, but their kids stay home, because they like it there. I know this, but I don't tell Marcel, let 'im think it's better without a dad.

— It's better without a dad, isn't it, I ask the kids who were beaten and I don't let it go until they say yes, it's better.

Last night we got really scared. We heard banging at the door and we all woke up, even Marcel. We armed ourselves to the teeth. Marcel had the small hammer we use for cracking walnuts and he sat down strategically by the bedroom door. Dan had two knives, one for slaughtering pigs, Dad had given it to him when he left, to protect us from enemies, and one from who knows where. I had a hatchet, which I keep under my bed just in case, and we made our way to the door. We convinced Marcel to guard the bedroom. You guard the money under the rug, our treasure, otherwise we won't have money for food or toys. He knows we can't live without money and it's what robbers and crooks are after when they break in, so he agreed to his important mission. Me and Dan went closer to the door, there was no more banging, but we heard strange rustling sounds. If Dan hadn't been with me, I would've fainted from fright. But I'm the oldest and I'm not allowed to faint just like that. We got to the door and didn't know what to do. Should we open it? What if it's some crook who wants to kill us? Should we go back to sleep? But how could we fall asleep with someone rustling something at our door at three at night? I put my ear to the door. I heard a dog yelping. But how could a dog have banged on the door so hard? Let's turn on the light. Outside we could hear something with a really snotty nose sniveling and crying. Let's ask who it is. Who's there? No answer, but we could hear the crying more clearly now. Aha, it's a child crying. I opened the door and saw a tired child, half-asleep, whimpering on our stoop. And dirty, what should we do with him. We didn't know who he was or why he came. Maybe he's one of those kids beaten up by their dad, who's been here before. But how did he get in when the gate's locked and why didn't the dog bark at him? Maybe it did bark, but we didn't hear because we were sleeping. Maybe we forgot to lock the gate . . . Well, it's a good thing it's a kid. We suddenly felt sleepy, we were about to fall asleep standing up. Dan went to bed, Marcel was already asleep on the floor, hugging the hammer, the way other kids hug a teddy bear.

I've never slept with a teddy bear, they have germs. One time I slept with the cat, when it had hidden under the bed and I thought it was outside. After I had fallen asleep, it got in bed with me. When I wanted to turn over, I felt something heavy on me, I wanted to push it off but then I felt its warm fur, it was sleeping and purring or snoring lightly and I let it stay, I didn't kick it out. But I didn't let it sleep with me more than that one time, because Lenuţa told me cats like to sleep on your chest and they smother you to death or their hair can get in your lungs and you'll die twenty years later.

I put the nameless child to bed on the couch, I covered him with a blanket and he fell asleep immediately.

❦

Of course children shouldn't be beaten. But sometimes I really feel like knocking them to the ground! I'm the only one who cleans in this house, I sweep, I wash the floors on my hands and knees, I work my butt off instead of going out to play too, or watching television or reading something recommended for twelve-year-olds! And Marcel comes in, as dirty as a pig, with an armful of slats covered in dirt and grass and he goes around with his sticks through the entire house, and then throws them down in the cleanest room! Where I had just swept and the floor was so clean you could eat off it! And he doesn't even play with them, he just leaves them there, because he gets another idea, another game or who knows what! I started yelling at him, I picked up the broom and rushed to hit him with it. And he, when he saw the big broom raised above him, put his little hands over his head and curled up, waiting for the blow. He looked so helpless to me. He didn't even understand why I was yelling and why I wanted to hit him, he didn't try to defend himself either, he has no one to go running to, neither mom nor dad. Me, his older sister, was going to beat him and I'm all he has, and Dan, who hits him all the time, even if he kisses him after that. And I stopped the broom midair and didn't hit him at all, not even a little bit. I tried to explain it to him, listen Marcelly, I swept for an hour while you were playing outside, look how clean I got it, and you with your sticks, which you could've played with in the yard instead of scattering every-where in the house, look what a mess you made.

I tried to explain to him that what he did wasn't good, it's not like the sticks would've disappeared if I had hit him. That's the right way to deal with kids, to speak to them gently. They're little, they want to play. Marcel understood that the danger had passed, the broom no longer hovered over him threateningly, he solemnly promised to do everything I asked him to, he even picked up three straws of hay off the floor, apparently he was cleaning up too. He said he wants to build a city. But why in the house, you don't build cities in houses. You build cities outside. So they won't get rained on and no one accidentally steps on them. I assured him that neither Dan nor I would step on his city and said that outside he could make a well for it, he couldn't do that in the house because there's no way to dig the hole. And we'd help him. Dan came too and we took the sticks outside, and then I had to sweep again. But I was proud of myself: I hadn't hit him. I did what was right and educational—I taught him. When I have kids, I'm going to teach them with a gentle spirit.

❦

Dan came home crying that the dog at the corner house almost bit him and he had to run all the way home. If you're afraid, the animal senses that and it keeps after you. I took some bread and went with my brothers to make friends with the dog that was loose. A dog used to chase after me, too, when I was little, but now I'm not afraid anymore and dogs wag their tails when I pass by them.

— Here doggy-doggy!

The dog had dug a hole under the gate, so that it could come out onto the street. It came when I called and got close to us. Dan threw it a piece of bread, then Marcel did the same. The dog was a tiny, skinny thing.

— Look, doggy, these are my brothers, don't bark at them anymore and don't bite them.

The dog waited for us to feed it all the bread, then it went back into its yard. It caught the piece Marcel had thrown at it in midair, as if it were at the circus, and left with it. I taught my brothers not to be afraid of caterpillars or frogs. I told them that some dogs are bad and bite only because they're afraid that you'll hit them. Still, it's better not to get too close to big dogs. People who are afraid first of animals, then of other people, come to fear even their own shadows, and end up getting sick. Fear is a sickness.

Parents don't always educate their children well. For example, the little Cotruță boy with the curly hair comes over to steal whatever he can, because his ma told him to. When I caught him and grabbed him by the hair, he cried, but not very hard. He said, if I don't bring anything back home, my mom will hit me even harder, she hits harder than you. A kid so little and ragged, mistreated and hungry. Okay, fine, go ahead and steal something, but so I can see it. He went straight for the toy tractor in the sand. Nooo, the kids will cry. Dan brought out a hoe from behind the house and looked at me, can he steal this? Yes, I nodded. Cotruța's mom will be more pleased with a hoe than a toy tractor. You can play with the tractor, and Dan will watch to make sure you don't steal it. Then I brought out some clothes and candy and even a headscarf for his mom. Because if dad will need the hoe, I'll tell him who I gave it to and where he can find it. Cotruța left with all kinds of goodies. His mom should work with that hoe, not send her kids to steal.

— See, I said to my brothers, like a teacher, how hard some kids have it, their parents drink wine all day and don't take care of them, they don't work, if it doesn't rain in the summer, none of their crops come up. Their kids don't have plaid sweaters and shirts from Italy, like Dan's, or a rain jacket, like Marcel's. Or toys, like the ones kids who are polite and well-educated have. These kids don't do well in school. They don't know that they shouldn't eat with their elbows on the table, they don't listen to their older sister. And they don't get to eat apple pastries.

— But they do eat sweet cheese pastries, Dan shot back, I know they have a cow. And they drink milk every morning. I want cheese and sour cream with sugar on top!

— We'll buy some tomorrow morning.

I know who to see about milk or cheese when I need some. Everyone now has a cow on their farm. Kids should be fed dairy products, which you don't even need to prepare much. You boil the milk and the food's done!

℀

———

33

Don't cry, we have work to do now. We'll make a schedule. Time for crying: eight at night. It's better this way. What if I were to start crying right when you're hungry? Or when the chickens and other animals don't have any water and they're dying of thirst. As if your crying were the most important thing in the world.

When Marcel wants to cry, I say to him, please, let's go shake the rug, or water the flowers. I find him something to do and say, right now you're working, you'll cry afterward. And he forgets to cry after. But sometimes he doesn't want to listen to me and he cries, expecting me or Dan to comfort him. We feel sorry for him, but if we come close to him and think about Mom, about Dad, we'll start crying too.

After I said we'll schedule time to cry, I forgot, but Marcel came in at eight on the dot one night, with photos of Mom and Dad, he set them down nicely in front of us right when a movie was about to start and said: Let's cry, it's eight o'clock!

— Put those photos back! we barked at him. Can't you see the movie's about to start? Only dummies and little snots cry! Real men suck it up and fight when things are hard.

The kid had gotten tired of listening to us and he disappeared with the photos. I went to see what he was doing and he was putting them back, muttering something. He was probably griping to the parents in the photos about what mean and cruel siblings he has, who don't care about their mom and dad, only about movies.

When Marcel started crying again, I asked him why he was crying. He wants mommy, he wants daddy. So he'd stop crying that he wants his dad, I took him to the other neighborhood to show him little Gheorghiţă's dad. Right when I knew he'd come home drunk and beat his son with a belt or a switch. Everyone

———

34

laughs at and hits Gheorghiță, who's only in second grade but walks hunched over like an old man, he's afraid even of his own shadow, he's skinny and unhappy. His dad cusses at him, yells so that you can hear it all the way down the street. A few kids had gathered to see what he would do to Gheorghiță now.

— See what a dad's like? You think a dad just pushes you in a swing all day long?

The last time Dad was home, he wrapped a long piece of wire around a stick and hung the other end around a thicker branch for a make-shift swing. He had Marcel sit on the stick and he pushed him into the air, the wire came off the tree and Marcel flew right into a heap of dirt. It's a good thing too, he could've landed in a worse spot, next to the heap of dirt was a pile of trash with broken bottles, old wires, and scrap metal. If he had flown into that, God forbid, who knows what would've happened to him. Dad asked me not to tell you and I didn't tell you, because you'd fight again. You can't even stay together for a week anymore, you're already fighting. You're the perfect married couple, with three kids, only when you're on different continents. Almost a model family. Especially for Christmas and Easter. Marcel wasn't hurt, he didn't cry either, he thought it was fun. And Dad actually picked up that trash, because I said I'd tell you if he didn't . . .

He was still whimpering that he wanted Dad. He wanted Dad to swing him on the swing. We promised him that we'd fix up a swing for him, because it's not hard at all, and we'll tie it to our walnut tree. But the wire wasn't strong enough, when we tried to wind it, it broke, and we couldn't wind the other wire we found around the stick either, it was really thick and I wasn't strong enough. In the end, we went over to Gheorghiță's fence. We stood by the fence and listened to the cussing, but we didn't stay to hear him get beaten, it was too hot and we got thirsty. Marcel was frowning the whole time. On the way back he told me that he's going to have three sons and he'll never hit them.

Never ever? What if they take all the candies outside, without their mom, dad, or other brothers having tasted even one? What if they come home without their bicycles? What if they drown all the ducklings in a barrel?

Marcel did all these good deeds last year.

The candies he had just wanted to show the kids outside, to brag, and one of them simply grabbed the bag from his hand, went inside his house with it, locked the door, and that was it, no more candies. Goodbye, "Joy" candies! The bicycle was taken from him by some kids at the other end of the village, Marcel didn't even know them, they asked him nicely to let them have a turn and they were off. Dad had to go through the entire village, looking high and low and asking about the bicycle, because it was expensive and almost new, Marcel had just learned how to ride it. The bike, in fact, belonged to Dan, who pulled Marcel's hair, he kicked Marcel in the butt, Mom could barely get him to stop. And when Dad brought the bike back, it looked like it had been through a war, scratched up, without its training wheels, without its bell and little light.

As for the ducklings, they had to, in Marcel's opinion, learn how to swim. Last year, my youngest brother drowned all eighteen ducklings, there had been twenty in all but two had died earlier. He went over to the barrel of water and propped a chair up against it. And when the ducklings were drowning, he couldn't even reach them to get them out of the water, he was too little. It's a good thing he didn't think to teach the chicks to swim. He had seen in some cartoon that ducks swim. And he said they were being lazy, they were sleeping in the water instead of kicking. And in just a few minutes, he had drowned them all. Mom didn't even scold me for not watching him. We were all at home.

You can find as many examples of bad dads as you want, they're pretty much all drunks who beat their kids. Even our dad hits us when he's home for a longer period of time. He pulled my ear in front of the other girls, and he chased Dan around with a wooden slat, yelling at him, when he hadn't even done anything.

I've never seen a bad mom. Maybe some of them hit their kids, but no one says my mom's bad and she hit me for no reason. There's only one woman drunk in the village, she has a pretty name, Luiza, and she drinks until she falls asleep on the street, next to fences, she pees herself and she stinks so bad that even the flies avoid her, not even they can stand the smell. And if you didn't know who she was when you saw her sleeping on the street, you might think she's dead. The woman is rather old and supposedly her husband left her for a younger woman from one village over, her kids forgot about her too, they don't come to see her anymore, to ask her, how have you been, Mom, or to bring her something good from the city. They've got their own homes, kids, cars, and they've forgotten about their mom. And she, out of grief, drinks and drinks, to forget the pain. Supposedly she was the village beauty. Maybe she was a good mom too, maybe she doted on her kids, who knows . . .

Sometimes, we go into the parlor and look at your dresses. On Sundays, sometimes, we put on a concert, we play family.

I wear one of your dresses, which fit me, they're a little big but next year they'll be perfect. Dan, who plays the dad, swims in Dad's clothes so he gave up putting on those oversized pants and shirts because he can't move in them and we die of laughter at how he swishes his floppy sleeves and how his pants fall down even though he's tightened his belt to the tightest notch. He makes do with a vest and that black hat which Dad has never worn, maybe he got it from his Dad too. We smell the clothes. The hat smells of Dad and the dresses of Mom. But most of the clothes smell like the tobacco and moth balls that were stuck in there to keep the moths away. Mom and Dad smell much nicer. Mom smells like Easter bread and pastries, Dad smells like milk, after he milks the goats, and hay, after he feeds them. Mama smells like noodle soup, and Dad like mushrooms, when he goes to the forest, he brings back lots of mushrooms, he dumps them out on a newspaper in the middle of the room and we pick out the prettiest ones.

And so on . . . And what do you stink like when you go pee-pee in your bed? You're a big boy! I don't go pee-pee, I sweat, Marcel says. But he only does that if he eats watermelon at night. It happened last year. This year the watermelons aren't ripe yet.

I don't know who Marcel resembles, he's so picky and complicated. First, he cried because he didn't have a toy car for a boy who comes over to play with him. Fine, okay, let's go buy you one from the store. And at the store, he started crying again. That if Mom hadn't gone away to work, we wouldn't have any money right now to buy him a toy car and other toys, but it would've been better to have Mom and no toys and he started wailing in the store, so the shopkeeper didn't know if I'd buy the toy anymore or not. I knew that if I didn't buy it for him, he'd start wailing again at home, that he wants the toy car, the exact one he saw . . . so I bought it for him. Then he stopped crying and played with the car. The kids that come to play with Marcel each want to have their own toy and when they leave, they want to take it home with them, they don't understand that it's not theirs. Let their parents go work too and buy them one. So I have to be on the lookout when they leave and not let them take our toys. Some even cry and I get so angry that I feel like giving each of them a kick in the butt so they'll have a better reason to cry. For real, do you see me stealing toys from anyone or does anyone give me anything for free, just for batting my eyes? I have to tear the toy, food, cat, out of their hands, I wait at the door with a broom and my brothers search them.

And Marcel starts crying because one of the three boys who come to play with him doesn't have a toy car. See what kinds of things I have to spend money on.

When Marcel was little, he had a stroller that Dan and I liked a lot. If our parents weren't around, we'd move Marcel onto the bed, we take turns getting into the stroller, we'd rock each other and push each other fast across the room, first me, then Dan, I don't know how that stroller didn't break . . . And Marcel waited patiently on the bed, he was a baby but he understood that we liked his stroller too, and he waited for his turn, for us to put him back in his stroller and rock him. We made sure Mom never caught us. I remember Dan as a baby too, with his little bandy legs, and look what big boys they are now!

❦

———

To try to seem like grown-up men, they say really bad cuss words. One time I was in the house with the window open and I heard everything they were saying. A boy with a dad, who could really give them an earful, had come over and every time he let out a cuss word, the others would immediately repeat it. And about a girl, even though she was in kindergarten, they said "that whore Lenuţă." They apparently didn't like any girl, one's hair was too short or too dark, another because she cries like a cow at the drop of a hat, because she's spoiled or fat or gets around. If you didn't know how little they were, you'd think they were a bunch of geezers who had been through the wringer. That's how they talk about girls, but just one longer look from a snot-nosed girl, and they melt immediately and become the slaves of those tramps, they'd give them the shirts off their backs. I almost beat one up for making Dan carry her buckets of water, two at the same time. I can barely carry one. Her mom had told her to water the tomatoes in their garden and why should she carry the water, she'll just go and find some stupid men to do it. And Dan carried them, huffing and puffing the whole way. 'Cause he's a man, he's strong, he has muscles. If I ask him, he won't lift a finger, because he's a little kid, he hasn't started school yet and he doesn't know how to write. But "that whore Lenuţă" or Viorică, taller than Dan by a head, skinny and full of roundworms and maybe lice too, knows how to wrap him around her pinky and make him her slave. I didn't know how to make him go home without upsetting him, the gentleman. I had to tell him that Mom was on the phone. He dropped the buckets in the middle of the street, he was red and huffing like a train. After Dan left, I told that Lenuţă that if I catch her bothering my brother again, I'd mess her up and make her straight hair curly for free! Let her carry her own buckets, it's not like she was going to give Dan any of her tomatoes for carrying her water. At home I gave Dan a talking to, and he promised that he wouldn't carry water for her anymore . . .

℘

When are we going to the vineyard to get some grapes?

They aren't ripe yet.

Now no one steals grapes anymore, like they used to. There aren't really that many drunks left in the village either. If you can find two, they're famous. Everyone has wine and no one to sell it to. Our fine, bright wine (as Dad calls it) remains in cellars, in casks, since it's cheaper than mineral water. People prefer beer, Uncle Ion says, because it's sweeter and doesn't give you stomach acid.

When I was little, I used to pick grapes and guard them all the time . . . Dad left me alone in the vineyard, next to the forest, only once, to guard the fruit. Mom had gone home to lock up the animals and feed the little ones, Dad had to leave to get something to transport the grapes. So I stayed guard there. And I wasn't scared. Actually, I wasn't scared for the first few minutes. Then any rustling seemed to be made by a monster. I was sitting by the baskets of grapes and imagining a group of robbers coming by, stealing all the grapes, putting them into a sack, and putting me into one too. I waited there for hours until Dad came with the tractor and we went home. It's not that nice riding in a tractor, it jolts and rattles you, your stomach and guts get all tangled up. Same as in a cart.

Dad would bring a cart from somewhere in the village to transport the harvest from the hill or to load up the garbage from

41

the animals. We didn't have our own cart. He would say to me: Put on your flowered hat. A year ago, he bought me a hat fit for a little lady, very pretty, blue-green with a bow in the back, and with a small bouquet of all kinds of silk flowers, also in back. After I'd put on my hat, he'd say: Let's go, my girl, I want to drive you around the village, so everyone can see what a beautiful girl I have. And first Dad would circle the center of the village about twice, he'd stop whenever he'd see anyone, they'd start talking and the person would ask: Is that your daughter? Dad would answer proudly: Yes. The person would reply: She's gotten so big. Next thing you know you'll have young men at your gate. And Dad: No, she still has more growing up to do, and school. And so on. Only after Dad had met with all his friends and he was done talking, would he say, should we go get those beans? And he wouldn't make me pick beans, because they were too dry and they'd scratch me, you take care of the horse, wait there patiently.

Now when Dad comes home he doesn't drive me around in a cart anymore. He doesn't even want a cart, he wants a small tractor, 'cause a horse's hard to take care of, but you don't have to feed a tractor. You lock it up and leave for three years or however long to make money in Russia. And my brothers are thrilled that they'll have a tractor, they're already bragging in the village about their dad's future tractor. Just another year or two and he'll buy himself one. I would've liked a horse better . . .

No one brings us fruit from the forest anymore, Dad used to bring us little barrel pears, small and very sweet, wild cherries, late apricots and peaches, plums and damsons, juicy apples and quince. This week I promised my brothers we'd take a trip to our vineyard. I remember a cherry tree and a sour cherry tree, maybe they still grow fruit. The sour cherry tree is right next to the road, and the cherry tree is in the middle of old man Pleşca's vineyard. We'll see if it produced any fruit and if there's any left. We have to be careful so he doesn't catch us, but, who knows, maybe this year the trees didn't produce anything or the fruit isn't ripe yet. The kids are thrilled, they'd eat even leaves. Maybe the grapes are ripe, or the green walnuts are ready to eat. Except that I don't know how to get them out of the shell. Mom and Dad used to get them out for us. And the walnuts first turned their hands green, then black, from the iodine in the shell . . . No one brings us fruit. If you wait for someone to take pity on you, you'll stay hungry. Everyone takes care of their own kids, their own families, and if you don't help yourself, no one will. We'll take water, bread, cheese, and cookies with us, we'll breathe in the clean forest air, and we'll remember the happy times, when we'd go there on a stroll with our parents. We'd be on a stroll, they'd be working.

⁕

Today I finally saw who's been stealing our sand. All the kids in the neighborhood would play in our sand. They'd build palaces, garages for toy cars, wells, cemeteries, or they'd simply bury their own foot or jump in the sand, they were at our fence all day long. For a while, I've been noticing that the pile of sand has kept getting smaller. There was almost not enough left to play with and the three of us decided to watch to see who it was. And late at night a man from another neighborhood, I didn't know his name, came with two buckets and a shovel which he left in the sand for when he returned, probably to not have to carry it twice. I thought to myself: He's absolutely shameless, fine, you take a bucket-full, maybe two, but not for days on end (we didn't notice that there was less and less sand in the beginning), until you take all the sand from someone's house . . . We followed him, to see where he lived. And what did we see, the man was building his house and why should he spend money on sand when he can take it for free from a bunch of kids! But other than follow him, what could we do? We'll tell on him to Dad, to Uncle. We'll hide his shovel. He's a full grown man, he seems strong, he'll beat us if we dare say anything to him. Next thing you know he'll kill us over a bucket of sand. Sand isn't that expensive, but it costs something to transport it, in a tractor or a car, you have to have money for gas. Dad had thought about his three kids, he thought that summer's coming, the kids should have something to play with, and someone too, because if we have lots of sand, the kids who don't have any come by and it's more interesting. If the sun's out, the sand gets hot, we won't catch a cold while we're playing. And Marcel likes to stay outside in the sand all day long and he's easier to take care of that way, you don't have to go looking for him in the tall weeds and shrubs.

One summer, I had to watch Marcel who had just learned how to walk. I put him down on a thick blanket and we, a few girls, started playing. We were taking turns with a jump rope, and after a couple minutes, one of the girls noticed that Marcel was gone. And off we went to look for him. We couldn't find him anywhere and we called all the kids nearby to help. It was almost like playing spies, Indians, scouts, we spread out in teams and raced to be the first to find the wounded comrade or the hidden treasure. The neighbor across the street had just started building his house, it didn't have a fence and his yard was all grass, and a bit further down was a plot with thick, tall weeds, which for us kids was like a forest, you couldn't even see adults if they went in there. Mom called them brambles and she was afraid they were full of snakes. I looked for Marcel there and I finally found him, eating from a fistful of soil, covered in dirt, he couldn't walk that well yet and he had mostly crawled through those weeds . . .

So Dad, being a thoughtful person, had brought us sand to play in, and that man stole it. I think he stole from other people, too, because where would he get any money if he lived in our village? And what could we do? The next day, we took our sand into the backyard, so he couldn't steal it anymore. I told Uncle what the thief looked like and where he lived. Uncle went over and talked to him, he said he didn't steal it, he just took two buckets of it because he really needed it, but he's waiting to borrow a car and he'll bring it back, he'll even unload an entire carful in our yard. 'Cause he doesn't take sand from the mouths of hungry children. His boy comes to play in our sand too and he's not heartless. But it's not like we eat sand . . . Uncle told us to tell him if anyone does anything bad to us. For now, we haven't let anyone get the best of us. But we don't belong to anybody, no one's like Mom and Dad. If Dad were home, that man wouldn't have stolen our sand. But the way it is now, they could steal even our fence, if they wanted to. What can three kids do? Because I, in their opinion, am a kid too.

I can't even imagine anymore what it's like to be at home with a mom and dad. For them to wash your clothes, clean the house, cook, and you to just goof off. I can't stand washing floors, for example. Friday, the day I clean everything, I had

Dan wash them, because I really didn't feel like it. Dan worked diligently, he was all sweaty, I praised him. But when I looked closely, all the walls were splashed. He, when he had wrung out the rag, had splashed water everywhere. I had to take a very clean rag and some soap and water, and wash the walls. But whitewash isn't washable paint, so I couldn't get the stains completely out and it'll stay like that until the next time we whitewash. If I had washed the floors myself, I wouldn't have struggled to work three times harder afterward. But could I really get mad at Dan? It's my fault, I shouldn't have exploited the kid. Women are the ones responsible for keeping a house clean. It isn't man's work. By the way, I'm surprised he even agreed to wash them, it's the first time he wanted to. And the last time I made him.

Kids kill flies, mice, and frogs. Frogs are useful, they eat flies and mosquitos, I told my brothers not to kill them. They can kill flies, but I don't like when they torture them. They tear off a wing or a leg and then watch them. Kids are mean and cruel. Dan and Marcel are mean sometimes too. If I leave them alone, they play together for a bit, then they start riling each other up and fighting as if they were a couple of dogs. I don't even know what to do with them anymore. They fight, they hit each other. Then they make up, they hug and kiss each other, and play with each other again. If some little boy comes by that they don't like, they kick him out. It's our sand, go away! They're my cars, don't touch them! I feel sorry for that little boy. When I was little and I wanted to play with someone, I would go over to two little girls who were sisters, neighbors of ours, who kept kicking me out, since there were two of them and they played together, they didn't need me. They would kick me out especially when they had something good to eat and they didn't want to share. And I wanted it so badly! They didn't want to give me even the cherries that were going bad on their tree. I would tell Mom, and she would ask their mom to give her some cherries for me. And the girls' mother wasn't as stingy as them and she'd give me some. Once I climbed up their tree by myself, secretly, but they saw me and they wanted to get me down with a long stick. Get down from our cherry tree right now! I told Mom who went and picked a little pail of them for me. I filled up my pockets with cherries and shot the pits at the girls from behind the fence. They couldn't see who was shooting at them. If they had seen me, they would've said: She's eating cherries from our tree and shooting pits at us! They would've complained to their mom, who would've complained to my mom, who would've scolded me. But no worries, after their cherries, it would be time for our apricots. And what apricots! I'd choose a ripe one, the most beautiful one I could find, as if an artist had drawn it, and I'd go out on the street with it, but I wouldn't eat it, I'd just sniff it, looking at it from every angle, until those nasty sisters died of envy. Let them ask their mom to come ask my mom to give her a couple of apricots for her precious babies. When their cherries were ripe, I'd tell them that we have apricots and plums, you're going to want some, but they would always tell me to go away. The apricot tree has grown big, but the plum tree produces fruit once in a blue moon and, when it does, the fruit falls off when it's still green. Unripe plums don't taste good, but we like green apricots. Except we don't eat our own, we take green ones from others.

We wait for ours to ripen. I wait, Dan not so much, I caught him right in the act. Marcel would've broken one off too, but he couldn't reach them, he was still too little. It's not good to have trees by your fence. Anyone who walks down the street can reach up and grab your fruit.

※

Sometimes I walk down the street and I really want to find something. If you search, you always find. Sometimes it's just a pretty button, it's a good sign. I keep walking down the street until I find something. I once found a man's comb, for short hair. A glove and a hairpin. I've found coins and one time a five lei bill. Dan and Marcel find things from time to time too, but they're only interested in things like toy cars and bicycles, and they bring home all kinds of little wheels, toy parts.

But I hate losing things! I never want to lose anything. I was wearing a butterfly clip, I ran down the street and when I got home, I remembered I had stuck it in my hair, and it wasn't there anymore, I had lost it. I looked for it down every street, even the ones I hadn't been on, maybe the wind took it, but it didn't turn up. I'm sure someone found it and was glad. Now I have short hair, because there's no one to do my braids for me. Every time Mom comes home, she gives me a haircut. It grows back even faster. I used to have really really long hair and Mom would wash it for me and rinse it with vinegar and herbs. I had a lot of hair too, thick and bushy. Mom said that only big girls wear their hair long and I'm not big yet. Rodica is a classmate of mine, her mom works in Italy too, but her hair is long, blond, and fine as silk. She braids her own hair. She can do two braids or just one, she can start the braid from the top of her head or from the bottom, she also knows how to do a French braid. I don't. I don't plan on learning either, since Mom had always done it. Maybe if I had a little sister, I'd learn by practicing on her hair, but as it is . . . Mom had a light touch, she didn't pull my hair.

Is it true that there, in very rich and developed countries, all the kids are good-for-nothings? They don't help their parents, they don't know what to do with their younger siblings, they don't know how to make food or milk a goat? A bunch of little leeches on their parents' backs! With dads, moms, nannies, teachers, the roly-poly ninnies let themselves be washed, fed, dressed, put to bed, woken up, educated.

At twelve years old, kids are really grown-up and responsible, they take care of other younger kids. When they're twelve, they don't cry that they want their mommy or daddy, they clean the entire house on Fridays or Saturdays. The little dummy splashed all the walls with the rag, so I'd never make him wash the floors again. But they grated apples until their fingers bled. And neither of them cried. And there was blood of theirs in the grated-up apples, but it was no big deal, it's not like that ruined them. They ate the pastries with their hands all bandaged up but they said it didn't hurt, they had bled so much that I used all the gauze we had on them. At twelve years old, I make pastries for my brothers. And we make sweet bread too, because it isn't hard, with leaves made of dough on top, for decoration. Dan eats all the leaves as soon as I take them out of the oven, while they're still hot. I get mad, but then I get over it. In any case there's no one to see how beautiful they are, not like it's

Easter so that we'd take them to church and the whole village could see. I never cry, what good would it do? We live well, we have enough food. We have a dog and a cat at home, a pig and chickens. We eat cookies with strawberry cream filling. I don't cry, but sometimes I feel like crying and then I want to hide in some corner, so my brothers won't see me. I know I've got no reason to, I've got nothing to cry about, I'm a big girl and I'm healthy, everything's going really well for me, and it's the same for my brothers, nothing hurts them, water doesn't drip from our attic when it rains, the way it does in the homes of other kids, who live with their dad and keep a bowl under the hole in their attic. Everything's good here. So what if I cry a bit sometimes for no reason.

※

Mom, do you remember when you asked one time how the cat was doing, about two years ago, right as our neighbor had just set it on fire and it was dying in terrible pain? And yesterday, when you asked about Dan, my heart started racing. Dan wasn't home, he said he was going to go play with some kids and he still wasn't back. After I spoke with you, I quickly went to look for him. I found him with some kids, I grabbed his hand and said let's hurry home, so nothing happens to you. After a couple steps, he started whimpering that he can't walk that fast, 'cause his leg hurts, he had fallen down. When I rolled up his pant legs, I got scared. He was all scraped up, swollen and bruised. He had fallen off a bike into a ditch, he could've gotten totally mangled! The bike, which he had borrowed from a boy, wasn't even scratched. He didn't have any other bruises, he had also skinned his elbow a bit. I put fleawort leaves on him and rubbed him with alcohol. And Marcel and I both blew on him so he'd feel better faster.

I really loved that cat! I brought it home one winter. I had found it, tiny and hungry, in an alley, and took it with me. Dad didn't say anything, but when it got bigger and became pregnant, he took all its kittens and threw them into the ravine. 'Cause we raise pigs on this farm, not cats. One's enough. I went to go look for them and the cat came with me, we both looked along the ravine, but we couldn't find a single kitten and we both cried. And some people say animals don't have feelings, that they have no soul. The cat had human eyes, sad and mournful. I'll never forget them. The second year, Dan, who was about four years old, was afraid that Dad would throw the kittens into the ravine again and he hid one in the washing machine, without telling us. The cat kept meowing next to the washing machine, but by the time we found the kitten, it had died of hunger. This time Dad left the cat the other two kittens, because I had found kids who needed a cat on their farm when the kittens got bigger, and Mom said it's not good to kill animals as if you were a common murderer. Don't you see how hard it is on the kids? The cat didn't know what we had decided and it stayed by its kittens to protect them from Dad. It would go get food and hurry back to its kids, are they still there, are they gone? Then it understood that no one was going to kill its kittens and it took them out from the attic, into the sun, in the garden, and it let them cuddle and play where we could watch. It was proud, see what beautiful kittens I have? One was brownish like its mother, and the other was white, only its front paws had little black stockings. When its kittens got bigger, it would bring them sparrows and mice. I noticed that it would give treats only to the brownish one, it wouldn't give anything to the white one. That one was visibly skinnier. It probably looked like its tomcat dad, who had betrayed the mom cat and had left her for a puffier, prettier cat. That's why the mom cat loved the one that looked like her more.

Sometimes, after talking to you, my heart feels so heavy! I want to cry, but as soon as I start tearing up a bit, these brothers of mine start wailing and I can't get them to stop. I can't even hide somewhere and cry in peace because my eyes get red and my head hurts . . .

Marcel comes in wailing.

— Hey, why are you crying?

— He hit me.

Who could've hit him, because I didn't see him playing with any kids, he wasn't out on the street, he's stuck like glue to us all day long, bothering us. Dan says he's got work to do and I have to ask him really nicely to play with Marcel.

— Who hit you?

— Dad.

Marcel knew I wasn't going to believe him, that I'd look at him as if he were out of his mind and he grabbed the hem of my dress and pulled me after him. He took me to our farthest off room, where it was cold and dark, and I saw. He had stuck a pillow inside an old coat of Dad's, on top of which he had put a hat that I knew was Dad's but which he had never worn, in any case I'd never seen it on him. Marcel's dad had boots and pants too. Marcel looked at me triumphantly, see, there's Dad, apparently. I picked up a stick (where in the world did he find one so long and thin), that's what Dad had hit him with, supposedly. I took the stick and swiped him on the butt with it.

— Like this?

— Yes, he said, and he didn't cry because I hit him.

— But what had you done?

— He had told me to feed the animals and I didn't, to clean up behind the house, and I didn't. You bum, he said to me. You're a waste of space.

These kids imitate everything.

"You're a waste of space, you bum!" Dad would say to our cat who asked for food and didn't catch enough mice. About not feeding the animals, he must have heard someone from the neighborhood talking about it, how could we make Marcel, who's so little, feed the animals? He doesn't even feed the dog, to make sure that the dog doesn't think Marcel's the main course and eat him too.

And behind the house, where all Dad's tools were scattered, no one steps foot there anymore. Mom, who'd clean up everywhere else, never went there, and she'd say to Dad: You didn't clean up behind the house! But now everything's organized there. Uncle comes by from time to time looking for a hammer and rummages through things, we don't touch anything.

Marcel often goes into the room with his dad and I hear him talking, fighting with him, then he simply curls up against the coat until he falls asleep. It's pretty chilly there and I wake him up, but he doesn't want to leave the room, 'cause he wants to stay with Dad. When Marcel asks me something and I don't know the answer, I tell him to go ask Dad. Then Dan messed up the dad. He got mad for who knows what reason and he hid the hat, he put the coat up on the hook . . .

That's it, I'm tired, I can't do it anymore! I feel like running away from home. Marcel loves it when I stroke his head, he sits quietly, he almost starts purring, as if he were a kitten. As if I had nothing better to do. But at night, when he doesn't want to eat or can't sleep, he expects me to caress him, so I've got no choice.

And since he kept dreaming about Mom making him breakfast, I, after seeing him build a dad, thought I'd make him a mom the same way. I put a dress on over a pillow, tied a headscarf over one of the corners, and the mom was ready. You want a mom, here's a mom. I put my hand through a sleeve, the way they do at the theater, look, Mom is pouring tea for her sweet little boy. Dan played along.

— Mommy, I'd like a little cup of tea.

But Marcel started showering the pillow with punches. I even spilled a bit of hot tea.

— I don't want tea from a pillow!

It completely ruined our mood. We had wanted to play, we thought it would make us feel better.

Next time, tell him three days ahead of time when you're leaving. To mentally prepare him.

Dan understands, he doesn't cry, I tell him he's a big boy, the way you told him too, that he's the man of the house, that any day now he'll be going to school, that he'll have the nicest suit, the nicest backpack, the nicest notebooks and everything else, that it's not for nothing that Mom goes to work and makes money, and Dad too, for us. I tell him he's almost taller than me, that he's smart, mature, and he understands our situation.

Actually, I don't know how much he understands, but when Marcel cries, Dan stops sniveling and helps me calm down the younger child. Because Marcel's capable of crying three days nonstop. He wakes up in the morning, Mom's not there, Dad's not there, and when he cries, it's as if he were singing. I think he likes hearing himself cry. As if he were one of those women hired to wail at funerals. He raises his voice, he lowers his voice. When his cries are high-pitched, they're like a goat's, when his cries are lower, in a deep voice, they're like those of a spoiled young ewe or ram that wants milk after it's already been weaned.

We stand there and can't do a single thing. We can only wait for him to fall asleep, hiccupping in his sleep. When he cries so pitifully, we listen from the room next door and I say to Dan: I'm strong, it doesn't make me cry when I hear him. Dan: Well, I'm even stronger. We stand facing each other to see who'll cry first. If something trickles down Dan's cheek: It's not a tear, I'm sweating, it's too hot. Sometimes Marcel comes in, with tears in his eyes, he looks at us and doesn't understand what we're doing, why we're glaring at each other.

Three-year-olds are amazingly smart. Afterward, as they grow up, they keep getting stupider. Marcel is often much smarter than Dan. Marcel hasn't learned the solutions to every problem and situation and he thinks on his own. When you start learning, you're given ready-made answers that fall into all kinds of categories, from here to there, but life doesn't have exact limits, and because not everyone, neither people nor animals, functions according to the same rules, that creates problems, gaps in communication. People don't think anymore, they memorize answers instead. My teacher didn't tell me this, I thought of it on my own. It's true that this winter Marcel stuck his butt against the stove door, the stove was barely warm, but the iron door, next to the fire, was already burning hot. How was he to know? After that, he came over and turned his bare bottom to us and begged, in tears: Blow, it stings. We weren't

———

dying to do that, but he was so burnt, and the skin on butts is so thin and delicate, that we blew very hard, so Marcel could hear how hard we were trying for him. He got a blister there and he couldn't sit or sleep on his back, the poor thing. It didn't leave a mark.

%

Someone is breathing heavily under my bed.

Mom, someone huge is under my bed and is fast asleep! I'm so scared I want to scream! The breathing stops when one of my brothers comes in and talks to me, or when I turn on the TV. I hear it only when it's quiet. Sometimes it stops, as if that giant had opened an eye, looked at me, shut it again, and gone back to sleep. I know there's no one under my bed but I feel a presence. One time I felt that same giant breathing when I went into the classroom and no one was there. I was the first one at school, the classroom was unlocked, I put my bag down on a bench and I listened to the silence for a bit. And I heard it. Maybe that's how the earth breathes. When I went to the vineyard one day by myself, I was walking through the clover barefoot and the soft grass tickled the soles of my feet, I felt the earth was a gentle, loving animal, that caresses me with everything it has, that gives me good things and loves me like a grandparent or a mother hugging her child. I listened to the earth and it was breathing. Then, on the road back, I wasn't afraid of anything. If a blade of grass had asked me something, I would've answered it without being afraid. I wonder if it's the earth breathing in our house or someone else. I don't want to be afraid anymore.

In our village, there's no boy as handsome as our cousin Lucian. He goes to high school in Chişinău, he's a city boy, he has dark eyes, thin eyebrows, red lips, and he's come to see Grandma before she dies, and to eat fruit and breathe clean forest air. He brought us treats from the city, most of them for us, because we're kids without parents. He's over our place the most, playing with my brothers. When we saw each other the first time, he put both hands around my waist and said, look, you're so thin that you fit between my two hands. It's because you have long fingers, I answered. But most of all I liked it when he put a couple fingers under my chin and stared into my eyes, exactly the way they do in movies, and kissed me on the cheek. Cousin, he said, and I felt myself getting all red as if he had said who knows what to me, and because I didn't want to blush, I blushed even harder. I was worried that he'd seen something on my face, that I hadn't washed my eyes well or that I had gotten a zit on my nose.

Then Lucian played with my brothers (he doesn't have brothers or sisters, he's an only child, like a prince) or he took them for a walk to some relative's, where they'd all eat and I'd have one less thing to worry about. Except that in the evening, when he'd bring them home, my brothers, who adored him, wouldn't leave him alone until he promised he'd come back. They'd ask him when and if he said, I don't know, Marcel would start wailing, until Lucian promised him he'd definitely come back tomorrow. Good job, brothers. I wanted him to come back tomorrow too, but I wouldn't have been able to convince him.

Two older girls, with boobs, came to our gate and asked

about him. He went back to Chişinău, I lied. I don't know if they believed me, but they said: Every girl has a cousin, you're not the only one. I think they live in Grandma's neighborhood. They smelled a man, the tramps. I didn't tell Lucian. Auntie Zina, his mom, asked us to pick her a pail of apricots for compote and jam. She'll give us some of the jam, and I hope Lucian will deliver it. We'll pick apricots on the last day, so they'll still be fresh when he gets back to the city.

Lucian invited all the cousins to the meadow to play ball. I would've wanted it to be just the two of us, or us two and my brothers. A swing was set up in the meadow and Lucian swung only me. Of course, the other girl cousins will say, it's because she doesn't have a mom or dad here or because she's going to pick apricots for him, but I don't think that's the only reason. Then everyone started playing ball, and the two of us went into the forest, so I could show him the spring with the cross. We sat down next to the water. After we drank a bit, he recited: Child, put your hands on my knees. I believe eternity was born in the country. When I put my hands on his knees, he forgot how the rest of the poem went. He thought for a second and said that his mom named him Lucian in honor of a great poet. Then he took my hands off his knees, as if they were too hot, and he said that I'd grown up so quickly, that he remembers when I was as small as Marcel and even smaller and he held me. I don't remember, but I'd like him to hold me now too. I couldn't even imagine myself as small as Marcel. As small as Dan, I remember what I was like then. I have my little dresses and I remember wearing them. I liked one especially, with nautical stripes. Then I showed Lucian what girls look like when they get older, he doesn't have sisters and he doesn't know. He asked me to, if I wanted to show him. He said my

chest pokes him, he twisted my nipples and he asked me if it
hurts. It doesn't hurt. I thought about the horns on a little goat
when he said that I poke. Then he went farther down, where he
took a longer look and it sent shivers up me. I didn't get to see
too much of him, because he was afraid the kids would come
and see what we were doing. He said he'd come over and show
me something, but because of my brothers, he hasn't shown me
anything, they don't leave him alone for a second. Only when
it was time to pick apricots, and both of us were in the tree,
did Lucian finally show me what he pokes with. My brothers,
since it was time to work, had run away to play and had left us,
finally, by ourselves. Give me your apricot, I handed him my
apricot, not this one. My apricot meaning my cheek, not the
kind we're picking. He pulled me onto his branch and kissed
me. We clung to each other for a long time, I would've like to
stay that way forever, I would've hung from that branch with
him my whole life, like a bird, like two birds. As long as it
doesn't rain. Then Lucian left. When he was leaving, he said
he'd come back. I told him about all the fruit we have in the
fall, it's all natural, no one's ever sprayed pesticides on them,
no one's been around to do that, and that he should come over
and pick some, why should he pay money for them in the city.
He said his mother doesn't allow him to stay in the village for
too long, because there are too many drunks and whores. He
also said there are a lot of bad boys and that I should watch out
for them. I should watch out, in general, for everyone, because
I'm so little. What do you mean I'm little? Look, I'm up to
your shoulder. Then Lucian took me in his arms and spun me
around, you're little and as light as a doll. You have to grow
up some more. And even though I was little and light, he still
kissed me on the lips, as if he had read my thoughts, I had

really wanted him to. It was the second time he had kissed me, the first time had been in the apricot tree.

Now I understand what all the talk is about. You can brag to everyone that you've been kissed, you can lie about it so that the girls in the class die of envy. But now I know what it's like and I won't even tell anyone. I feel fulfilled and I'm almost all grown-up.

℀

For Marcel being grown-up means being as tall as Daniel. Right now he thinks he's little only because Dan's a head taller than him.

For Dan being grown-up means being as tall as Dad. Dan grows really quickly, he's getting longer and longer. At first, I thought his pants, from so much washing, were getting shorter. I told Mom that the material wasn't good. Maybe his pants are getting shorter, but Dan's legs are also getting longer, Mom said. Our boy's growing. His arms aren't getting longer as quickly. They outgrow his shirts more slowly. His shirts all fit. I caught Dan trying on one of Dad's shirts.

For me being grown-up means bleeding once a month. Three girls in our class have started already, maybe others as well, but they're ashamed to admit it. Girls who have their period are different. They don't jump rope at recess anymore, they hold onto their bellies importantly, and they look down on us, as if they had grown up twenty years in a month. They're not girls anymore, they're women. One got hers when she was eleven. And I'm already twelve and my chest has barely puckered. I want to be a woman faster. I bought a lot of cotton and put it aside. When Mom came home last time, she brought a packet of special pads, she said, for women. I think it was for me, for when it's time. I didn't want to open the packet, I wanted to wait, be patient, I told myself. I was afraid that if I opened it, dust would get inside and they wouldn't be sanitary anymore. And why should I waste them? Then I opened it and inside were lots of teeny tiny packets, all sealed. I opened one and I really liked it. How its little wings unfolded, how it smelled of chamomile, how it stayed whatever way and for however long you wanted it to. I can hardly wait to stick one inside my underwear.

Girls with big breasts say they work hard and that's why their breasts are big, from the physical exercise. But it's not true! With all the work I do, I should already have jugs like Veronica's. Two milk jugs that you have to haul over your shoulders, the boys laugh at her. I don't want jugs down to my belly button.

Mom doesn't send us toys, Dad doesn't either. Money for food, necessary clothes, from natural fibers, soft wool or cotton, bought second hand or hand-me-downs from the kids where she works, a few sweets. So we don't become obese, 'cause you can't cure that with any diet and kids who get fat automatically come down with two or three other conditions. But other kids receive beautiful and very expensive clothing, they come out to play in them and, in a few days, they've transformed them into rags fit for tying up a calf. A boy in my class received a cell phone from his dad. We watched him out of the corner of our eye, he would listen to music during recess and write messages while the teacher was talking. The other boys envied him, they asked to see his phone and they dropped it a few times, on accident, until it didn't work anymore.

At the end of last year, for the New Year's concert at the school, Mom brought me a princess dress. It was so beautiful, it was as if I were a queen among servants and other common mortals. I was also chosen queen of the ball, everyone praised my dress, I spun around in it and I danced. Only once I got home did I see that it was full of holes made by a lighter. I hadn't felt a thing, I don't know who had burned my dress. All around me only smiling, admiring faces.

Mom got scared that the whole dress could've caught fire and something could've happened to me. She told the principal, but what did the principal know about it, she said all the kids from the entire school had gone to the ball, we were playing, all crowded together, you wouldn't know who to blame. Since then, Mom doesn't buy me clothes that are that beautiful anymore, so I don't stand out.

※

I got a bag of walnuts down from the attic in the evening and I had the kids help me crack them and get them out of the shell. Tomorrow morning we'll eat bread with walnuts and cheese. Our money ran out and we'll get more only on Thursday. Today is Monday, so three days of eating walnuts in the morning and potatoes for lunch and something for dinner, we'll see what. We might boil, for example, macaroni.

In the morning, the dog receives its portion of bread and walnuts. Its portion is smaller, because it's smaller as well. The dog eats the walnut first, then the bread. We give it the entire walnut, to break it open by itself and take out the meat. That takes longer so the dog will think it's eating more. It doesn't want cabbage. The cat, however, likes it, the cat chews on it, nibbles it, sucks on it, until there's nothing left. Animals need vitamins too. Then after bread and walnuts, the kids also receive a slice of bread and jam, the dog doesn't get dessert, because we're almost out of jam too and who knows if Mom will make more, if she happens to come this fall. I don't know how to make jam. This little jar already is from an aunt, who said her family doesn't really eat jam, she makes a lot, but a year or two go by until they open one, and it just sits there, then she throws it out. But she only brought us one little jar, as small as can be, where did she even find one so small. That cheapskate. Lets it get moldy, but she won't give it to others.

Aunt Vera is baking pastries right now, but she shooed us out of the house. We're dying for some pastries! She said: I'm making pastries and I'll send Lia to bring you some. We're all sitting at home and waiting. I'm positive that Lia will eat some of the pastries on the way. Or her mom will give her just half a small pastry, not even big enough to nibble on with one tooth, for us three hungry, insatiable monsters.

Marcel was waiting out on the street and came in to tell us when Lia was still on the way, she had barely turned the far corner, she was in a big hurry to brings us the pastries before they got cold.

— Go wash your hands, who knows how many germs you picked up while you were playing.

I wiped down the table and took out the sour cherry compote which I had made myself and I poured it into mugs. Lia showed up, out of breath:

— They're still hot, there are cheese, potato, and pumpkin ones.

And she undid the kitchen towel they were wrapped in. I saw there were a lot of them, we'd get full. They were already cut up, hot and soft.

— Do you want one?

— No, I already ate at home and Mom said not to eat any, because she'll make me more, and you don't have anyone to make you pastries.

— But you can have some sour cherry compote, right?

The kids ate silently, concentrating on keeping the food on their plates, they ate bent over the table so that they could gobble up any crumb that might fall, because if it reaches the ground, you can't put it in your mouth anymore. I gave each of us three big slices, and we'll eat what's left over tomorrow. I thought about what secret hiding places still existed in the house, where I could hide the rest of the pastries until tomorrow. Then I gave Lia back the towel and the plate after I had washed it. Tell Auntie thank you very much from us, the pastries were really good, we licked our fingers.

✻

No one brings us food when we're craving something or when we need something. Remembering the pastries we had received and eaten, I tried my hand at baking them. It's not that hard.

Mom had described the stages and procedures to me. The kids, hungry for pastries, offered to help me and they did everything I told them to. They grated the apple. They mixed the flour and water, and I threw out the lumps. I waited for the dough to rest for fifteen minutes, then I divided it into smaller hunks which I rolled out, I sprinkled grated apple on them, and the boys folded them up. Then I put everything into a pan of hot oil and that was it. My brothers enjoyed making pastries more than I did. We were all covered in flour. And I didn't even wait for the first pastry to cool off completely before I popped it in my mouth. I ate the second one quickly too. I finally ate the third one a bit more slowly. I fried the other ones by myself, the boys, now that their stomachs were full, had gone off to play. I didn't even need them. They ate so many! I don't want to brag, but my pastries were much better than all of my aunts' pastries. Except that it really tired me out, I don't think I'll be making more any time soon.

Our magnificent apples sometimes drop on the ground. Will any of them be left by fall? Dad says they should've been sprayed, but if you spray them, they aren't natural anymore. But if you don't spray them, they all drop on the ground and our pig munches so many apples that I'm surprised it doesn't get a bellyache. Lia says they feed apples to their rabbits and the rabbits' meat is very tender and sweet, as if you were roasting them in sugar. But I don't think the pig meat will get sweeter from these apples because they're not at all sweet yet.

❦

I have a secret that I've told only to Mom and Dad, not to my brothers: a pair of swallows have built their nest right inside the chicken coop. I didn't see them building their nest, when I discovered it, the swallows already had four chicks. One day, I heard some strange noises coming from inside the coop that weren't like anything I had heard before. I listened more closely: the chicks were clacking their beaks from hunger, calling their parents. Then one fell out of the nest and I saw only three beaks open wide, waiting for food. The parents both would lug flies to their kids all day long. I scanned the entire sky, as far as I could, to see if they had gone away from their chicks—not a swallow in sight. I'd go inside the coop, and at first the chicks always had their beaks wide open. Later they were curled up in

65

their tiny nest, you couldn't even see a feather, how did they fit inside there when they were already such big chicks? The coop isn't that tall and I can reach up to the nest. They've started learning how to fly now, it's no coincidence that the fourth one fell from the nest and the chickens ate its tender little flesh. Whoever thinks chickens eat only grain is completely wrong, they also eat tiny fish, and newborn bunnies, if they find a hole in the rabbit's cage and they can pull out one of the tiny animals with their beak. I never did a thing to the little chicks, I would only pet them with a finger, I would touch their tiny heads, and they wouldn't even make a sound. Then I would quickly leave. Each time, the mother swallow was waiting outside for me and would fly back and forth threateningly, you'd think it had three baby dragons, not three little swallow chicks. It wasn't at all afraid of me, even though I was much bigger than it, and if I had taken a chick, it probably would have pecked me, and grabbed it out of my hand or at least tried to. I don't want to harm or upset it in any way and that's why I didn't tell my brothers about the nest and I'm not going to tell them, so they don't secretly go and pick up a chick and drop it. There are fewer and fewer swallows left, they're hardworking and make a home for themselves, but the shameless sparrows chase them off and take over their nest. When Dad was home, he would chase off the sparrows from the swallow nests, he wouldn't let them settle there, but this year, since there's no one to take care of them, the swallows made their home with the chickens, where the stupid sparrows would never think to go in. Except that in the evenings I shut the coop door so rats or hedgehogs don't get in and steal a chicken, but I open it back up in the morning. And both parents or just one is waiting on the telephone wire for me to hurry up and open it so they can see and feed their chicks. I think they know which window is mine and that's why they sing so insistently until they wake me up. But they sing beautifully, I don't get mad. I'm not mad at the sparrows either, but they eat all the grain and all the chicken feed, all the seeds you plant in the earth, and tree blossoms, even the dog's food, as much as is left of it. Dad says we have to chase them off.

But worse than the sparrows is when the starlings descend, they eat everything, the way locusts do. I only saw a locust once. It was dead and very beautiful, it looked like a big grasshopper, but more colorful. Now the birds in the forest don't have much left to eat and they come to the village, you see all kinds of beautiful ones especially around the homes of old people who I think don't shoo them off or maybe the birds sense they're not dangerous. Two very small birds with long pointy tails and brown and gray spots on their stomachs made a nest at Grandma's. Grandma can't see well anymore, but when I described what they looked like to her, she said that they had to be wrens. She said she's heard them singing. A woodpecker hangs out in our trees. There are lots of them, almost every yard has its woodpecker. The village is full of woodpeckers. Sometimes a crow flies by and our rooster lets out a drawn-out squawk, as a warning, and the chickens hide wherever they can. I don't think that a crow could eat a chicken. More likely the rooster is making itself seem important, apparently it's vigilant and hardworking.

One evening, a cat came by our house. More used to come, our farm was big and there was food enough for all of them. I mean, cats go where there are mice, mice go where attics are full of grain, walnuts, corn, and sunflower seeds. Since our parents went away, we don't have anything left in our attic, so the mice don't really have anything to nibble and the cats don't have anything to catch. But if a cat comes to our house on its own, and it likes it here and doesn't leave, that means it's ours. We feed it and take care of it, Marcel will even give it a bath if we aren't watching him. But now we don't really have anything to feed it. We buy milk or receive it a liter at a time and we don't waste it, and we don't eat food with bones in it that often, and if we happen to have any bones, we give them to the dog, not to the cat. I was surprised when this cat showed up and allowed Marcel to ruffle its fur. There are people around with cows, sheep, with lots of food.

Now I finally understand. It came to eat the swallow chicks. I caught it prowling around the door of the coop. Then I heard the swallow parents screeching. When I heard their screeches, I already knew that the cat was there. I'd take the cat and tell it, you've got no business here! Leave the chicks alone! It would listen very obediently, stroll through the garden for ten minutes, watch me to make sure I didn't see it, and then it would go back to the coop. And the swallows would screech again. The cat probably couldn't figure out how I knew what it was up to. And since the swallows saw I could drive off the danger, they'd fly close to me or come to the window where I was sitting inside the house and screech that they were in grave danger, they wouldn't sing beautifully the way they did mornings. And how could I not go when they called me, begged me, for help? What else could a couple of teeny-tiny birds do when faced with a huge strong cat, that was hungry, because it definitely wasn't getting full on the crumbs from off our table. The three swallow chicks wouldn't fill it up either, but it's easier to catch them than to hunt fat sparrows that don't let you catch them just because you feel like it. And the mother swallow never gets tired of lugging flies for her chicks, which that wily cat wants to eat! And the mother swallow struggles so much. The mother and father both, in fact, I always see them bringing their chicks flies in their beaks, from morning to night. After I pick the cat up, they immediately quiet down and go looking for more food.

I'm so mad at this cat. It won't leave these chicks alone until it eats them. I know how cats are! Now it's trying to get the chickens used to him being around. The cat's hunting on chicken territory, and the rooster doesn't care for it, it comes up to the cat and pecks it right on the top of its head, it's really funny. I also saw a chicken peck its tail, probably to see what it tasted like, right when the cat was carefully pacing there, sniffing around.

The cat suddenly seemed to me to be a sneaky, lying animal, always trying to take advantage of others. I shut it up in the shed, with some food and water. I spoke very nicely to it, so it wouldn't be afraid of me and I could catch it when I needed to. When the cat came to us, it was already a grown-up cat. Didn't it have an owner? Why did it come to our house, of all places? With its fleas and all, which it would bring into our house and we'd never be able to get rid of them! With diseases and all kinds of germs, because who knows what kind of conditions it lived in before. With the ugly habit of climbing onto the table with its little unwashed paws and stealing whatever might be there, even something it wouldn't like, that it would then drop, which I would then have to pick up and throw to the pigs.

So, it didn't like salami, or cookies with strawberry cream filling, I don't know if it likes pastries, because I haven't given it any, we have to eat too. And then I always have to be careful so it doesn't get inside the house and steal something, so it doesn't open the refrigerator door with its paw, so it doesn't hide at night in my brothers' room and sleep on their chests and suffocate them. I could put up with all this, but I can't stand around all day guarding the swallows' nest. But I can't abandon the chicks either. In a week, they'll learn how to fly. An opportune moment for this goddamn cat. I can't even relax at night, I can't open the doors to air out and cool the rooms in this heat. As if I had nothing better to do than take care of this cat.

I tried to drive it away, to stop feeding it. But it has already studied the entire farm and it hides where I can't reach it, under the hay, in the garden, up in the attic. And if you kick the cat and drive it away, it won't let you pet it afterward, or catch it and take it away from the coop. So for now I shut it up in the shed. I'll keep it in there for a day or two, but then? Cats don't belong in there . . .

Then, it has to be carried off from the house. If it won't leave by itself, I'll take it. Dad took cats away before, there was one he kept carrying off and it kept coming back, and Dad nicknamed it "Lăpuşneanu" for the famous prince who told the nobles, "If you don't want me, it doesn't matter, I want you . . ."

I'll catch it, I'll put it in a bag with a zipper, and I'll quickly zip up the bag and take the cat as far away as possible. If it has its own house, it can go back to where it came from, if it doesn't want to, it can stay at a farm that's more promising than ours . . . Done. I opened the shed door and here kitty kitty, pretty kitty, hungry kitty, come here so I can give you some food. The cat meowed, it swished the tip of its tail, as if it could smell a potential danger with its tail, and it came closer. It let me catch and pet it, but when I went to zip the zipper after I had put it in the bag, it sprang out and disappeared. I had no clue it was that strong. I should've had Dan help me, I would've put the cat in the bag, and he would've quickly zipped it up. But I hadn't wanted to tell them that I'd be taking the cat away. If they had noticed its absence, I'd have told them it had gone back to its owner and its own house. Marcel pulled the cat's tail and it scratched him. He could've gotten an infection. Mom, on the phone, from the very beginning, had told me that we don't need an animal contaminating us. And she agreed that I should take it away. I had wanted to tell Marcel that the cat went home to its owner because it got mad when Marcel pulled its tail. I'll have to tell them that I want to take it away from here and that they'll have to help me and that's it! We'll all catch it and take it back to where it came from.

I didn't make it suffer, the way Ștefănel did with his dog. I caught it and Dan helped me. Marcel felt so sorry for the cat, which was meowing like an idiot, that he almost started crying. We walked down the road toward the school together and we dumped out the bag into a garden. Then we counted how many pretty houses there were on that side of the village and how many wonderful and rich new owners the cat had to choose from.

We walked back home slowly and I was afraid that the animal might get home before us. But it hadn't come back, it wasn't here on the second day either. It came back the third day, when I called Marcel to come eat, he was joyfully hugging the cat, probably promising it eternal friendship and territorial non-aggression. This time I left it alone. In the meantime, the swallow's nest had been deserted. The three swallow chicks the cat had been dreaming about had been eaten by the pig.

The very night we took the cat away, it started sprinkling. Raining and raining. It's summer, it's hot out, and the earth needs water to produce fruit. It's been raining for two straight days. I was worried about the swallows. The flies had hidden themselves. What will the parents and chicks eat? I saw the mother swallow huddled against the wind, under an eave of the house, it wasn't singing at all, and the chicks were screeching. I hoped they wouldn't die of hunger. If only the rain would hurry up and stop, so the flies would come out into the sunlight! I felt really sorry for them . . . I had seen how big they had gotten, they'd be flying any day now, they needed even more food than before. I had gone through the entire house looking for flies, so I could catch a couple and go feed the chicks. In the house, I found only one fly, the big, fat kind, I chased it over to the window and caught it. Then I found a few more in the shed, it's warmer there than outside and the flies were napping in the warmth and buzzing quietly. Some of them were standing still on the wall. I put as many flies as I could into my hand and went over to the swallows. The mother swallow was in the nest and it flew out when I came inside. The chicks weren't screeching at all anymore and I couldn't see anything. I waved the biggest fly over the nest, but not one beak opened up to eat it, then a chick poked up and opened its beak wider than its head and, gulp, down went the fly. I tried to stick the other flies straight into its beak, but I missed sometimes and a couple fell into the nest, and I don't think the chicks will find them, since they're used to being fed straight from their mother's beak, they're not going to look for food themselves in their nest. The mother swallow was out in the rain waiting for me to leave. Compared to the mother, the chicks were kind of ugly, but maybe they'd grow out of it. Meanwhile, the father turned up too, it was bigger and had a longer tail. They were both waiting and watching me. Dan came too, curious about what

I was doing. I wanted to show him the nest, but I changed my mind. I heard a chicken clucking and I came to look for the egg, but it's still too early. Not an egg in the coop. Look at the little birds, Dan said, pointing to the swallows.

Yes, these are swallows, they visit only good people and well-behaved children. It's really hard taking care of two kids when it's raining. I don't know what other games to play. Outside, it's rainy and cold. In this kind of weather, you feel your parents' absence more sharply, you miss them more intensely. I wanted to have the kids catch flies too, it would've given them something to do, but then I'd have to tell them the secret and the rain will stop eventually, the swallows will catch flies by themselves, it's better if I don't tell them. I turned on the TV and nothing interesting was on. We had already gotten bored with our toys, we searched through the closet for our fall clothes and got all bundled up so we wouldn't shiver from the cold, and we waited by the phone. It wasn't Saturday yet, but it seemed like the best thing we could do now would be to talk to Mom on the phone. Maybe she'd sense that we were thinking of her and call us.

The next day, in the morning, I went outside to see if the cat had returned by any chance. I even called to it very gently, here kitty kitty, but I got no meow in reply. I let the chickens out and then scattered grain for them. I gave them fresh water and they gathered around to drink. Outside, it was very cool for the middle of summer, the rain had stopped. I fed the pig and the dog, we ate too, we played a bit. The sun had come out but the sand was chilly, I didn't let Marcel build his palaces, so he wouldn't catch cold. I went over to the swallows, which weren't screeching. I couldn't see anything in the nest and thought I should stick my hand inside to make sure the cat hadn't stolen them.

The nest felt empty, the first thought that flashed through my mind was that the cat had eaten the chicks! I felt some more inside the nest and found the chicks, cold and motionless, I put them into the palm of my hand. They were dead. All three of them. I came out of the coop and saw the swallow silently sitting on the wire. I cupped my hands over the chicks, thinking that maybe if I warmed them up, their hearts would start beating again. I held them for a long, long time, then Dan came and he said let's warm them up with a hot water bottle and cover them up. That's how I would warm up Dan's feet in wintertime. Marcel didn't see any of this. The chicks had become moist in my hand and it seemed to me that the smallest one, the one in the middle, had gotten its heartbeat back. I was happy. They weren't dead. They'll come back to life, I'll put them back in the nest . . . but what if the swallow had left? If it had seen the empty nest and had gone away? Then we'll catch flies for the little chicks ourselves. I'll put my brothers on the job, we'll manage with three chicks that are this little. Yes, I felt the smallest one in the middle's heart beat. Dan poured the hot water into the bottle. I carefully set the chicks on the bottle so they wouldn't roll off and I wrapped them in a cotton kitchen towel. I spoke with my parents on the phone. Mom said to ask Dad about the chicks. Dad said that the chicks won't come back to life and that the swallow will lay another set of eggs and three or four more chicks will hatch. It's barely the middle of summer. But if it doesn't lay them, that means the summer will be very short. I should feed the chicks to the pig, not to the dog or cat or they'll get used to bird meat. After a couple hours I remembered to check on the chicks, but I saw only the bottle, Marcel had wiped himself with the towel and scattered the chicks, without seeing them. I picked them up off the floor. My eyes were very red from crying so much and I looked very ugly. I took the chicks out to the pig, it was noon and the pig was sleeping, it didn't even move, it wasn't at all curious to see what I had thrown to it. Then I went to see if the swallow had left or if it was going to lay new eggs. Maybe I shouldn't have thrown the chicks to the pig, maybe the mother would've warmed them up with her wings and they would've come back to life. Dad said they died of hunger or from the cold. When I saw the swallow near the nest, I thought that maybe I should've put the chicks back, to let it decide the fate of its children by itself. Maybe I shouldn't have gone so often to its nest. Maybe it hadn't fed them because of me, maybe it hadn't kept them warm because of me.

The cat came back that same evening. I think it had been looking for Marcel, who was very happy that his four-legged friend had returned.

After I gave it some food, the cat went over to its favorite spot, the chicken coop, as if it were getting paid to guard the swallow's nest. The swallow screeched again, I heard it, but I didn't go over. What would be the point? There aren't any chicks in there now, I have no one left to save. The cat stayed there all day, it would go to Marcel from time to time and meow that it wanted food, and then go back to the coop. Because of the cat, the swallow would be afraid to have more chicks. How could it, when a danger that size was stalking the swallow night and day? What else could I do to chase the cat away? I took the broom and yelled at the cat: Didn't I tell you to stop sneaking around here? Didn't I tell you to go home? And I went to hit it, but cats don't stay still so you can hit them, they run. I still landed a couple swats on its back.

Uncle came by and I told him about the cat. He said he had some mice or rats in his attic and he's been searching for a long time for a cat like ours. And if we don't need it, we should give it to him. Marcel got sad, but Uncle said that if you ever miss it too much, you can come over and play with it. It'll come back, because it already came back once. I'll feed it milk and cheese for three days and it will never step foot in your yard again, Uncle answered. I told Marcel that the cat had to be fed well, and it would die of hunger at our house. Don't you feel sorry for the cat? Uncle will feed it milk, we don't even have goats anymore, or a cow, or sheep. If you want a cat, let's bring our goats back home, you'll take them out to graze every day, you'll milk them every evening, carefully, so you won't get a hoof to the mouth, and we'll give the cat milk. Marcel petted the cat a couple more times and then, without saying a word, gave it to Uncle.

❀

Little Grigoraş's mom hasn't sent him any money for a long time. In summertime, Grigoraş would steal from people's gardens. If they'd catch him, they'd yell at him, pull his ears, a kick in the butt sometimes, sometimes a lash across his back. A man with a cart caught him and lashed him with a whip that stings really bad, but no one stopped to think that Grigoraş wasn't stealing because he had it so good, but because of hunger. And no one would die if two or three vegetables went missing. We, too, stole corn, which we boiled. Just two times, when we were really craving some. In the city, you can buy whatever your heart desires. But who in the village would bother selling you raw corn?

So we went to the vineyard, supposedly to get some more grass for the chickens, to see if the grapes had ripened. We left Marcel to stand guard on the road and, whenever he saw anyone, to blow the whistle we had gotten especially for occasions like this. He was supposed to whistle and run to our vineyard. Dan helped me break off the ears of corn. When they're wrapped in their husks, you can't tell if they're good for boiling or not, that's why you have to break off several, and whatever isn't good for us will be good for the chickens or the pig. I boiled three for each of us and salted them a little and, boy, did we eat them up . . . What deliciousness! We have our own cornfield and if it weren't so far away, we would've taken some from there. Dad gave our plot to people who bring us some of the kernels, a part of the harvest, but not very much, because the labor and the seed costs more than the harvest brings in and it's not worth the investment. And sometimes the drought's so bad that what you put into the earth doesn't even come up and you end up in the red. Before, on the way to our vineyard, as far as the eye could see on both sides of the road were crops, well-tended fields, now you see just empty land. You have no one to steal an ear of corn from. Our vineyard is also full of thick couch grass and sow thistles. I've picked orange poppies, too, from our vineyard. I also found a red poppy, but I didn't pick it. I left it so that it would produce seeds for more poppies.

Ştefănel doesn't have his parents with him either, for the past several years his grandma has been raising him. He's crazy now, his dog visits him. He offers it bones, but the dog doesn't want any, because ghosts never get hungry. Ştefănel asks it nicely, he cries in his sleep at night, and during the day, when he's awake, he says to the dog that only he sees: Take the bone! Even though it has forgiven him, the dog doesn't take the bone.

Ştefănel went crazy because of his own wickedness. He wouldn't let anyone get near his dog while it was alive. Not even his grandma was allowed to feed it. He said he'd be the only one feeding it. Then he'd call the kids over for a dog concert. What would happen there, I don't know for sure. Dan went one time, and when he came home, he couldn't stop crying. When I asked him why he was crying, he said that he felt terrible for Ştefănel's dog. Ştefănel tortures it with a bone. He keeps it hungry, he gathers up a bunch of bones or just one big juicy bone and waves the bones under the hungry dog's nose. I could imagine what the end of the concert was like: the dog loses hope of ever getting the bone, it goes into its cage and cries like a human. But Ştefănel still wouldn't take pity on it, he wouldn't give it anything and he wouldn't let any other child feed it. The kids felt sorry for it and they'd throw it bones or pieces of bread over the fence at night. But, more often than not, the food wouldn't land next to the dog and the dog struggled even more to try to reach it. If he caught his grandmother giving it food, Ştefănel would take everything back, as much as was left, he'd spill out the water and yell at his grandma. Supposedly he was training, educating, disciplining the dog, and no one was allowed to butt in. And afterward, when "the concert's over," he'd say: Fine, come get the bone, here's your bone, Rex! And the dog's eyes would light up with a kind of hope or gratitude, the dog would think about coming out of its cage and, if it came out, timidly, cautiously, Ştefănel would always hit it again, with his foot, or a switch, and Rex would barely manage to get back inside. At that moment, the more soft-hearted kids would burst into tears and go back home, and Ştefănel would yell after them: You little snot-noses! You girls! Bedwetters! And if it didn't come out of its cage, he hit the dog with his switch inside the cage until it came out, so he could hit it more easily.

All you have to do is climb up on the roof of a shed, that's not even as high up as the one on the house, to realize how small kids are, but so are grown-ups, they look like a bunch of tiny animals, itty-bitty and insignificant. What right does a child have to torture a dog, what right? It's small too, a bug there on the face of the earth . . .

The dog was getting skinnier and skinnier. A little girl told the grandma that the dog would die of hunger and that she'd beat Ştefănel to death. The grandma told her to take care of her own animals and not to worry about the entire village. And at school they say that they held a meeting, where they criticized Ştefănel for making our friends, the animals, suffer. That it's not nice, you have to take care of them, be compassionate, give them food and water, because they're chained up, they love us and depend on us. Ştefănel said that he saw on TV that that's how you train dogs so that they'll become real friends who protect people, and their dog is very bad and it would eat people if he didn't educate it. That there are people who beat and kill each other, parents who beat their kids worse than he beats his dog, and no one holds a meeting to criticize them. His mother taught him to say that, but it isn't true that their dog is that bad and that it eats people. It's actually very obedient and it looks at you with the eyes of a human who's in pain. Then Ştefănel called all the kids, come on, give it bones now! The kids held out the bones, but the dog didn't want them. It didn't even leave its cage. Ştefănel had taught it to eat only while he was beating it, meaning if you want food, you'll get beaten, if you don't want food, you won't get anything. And the dog was afraid to eat. Ştefănel fluttered his switch around, go on and give it bones, dummies! A kid threw a bone at it and the bone hit the dog right on the head. Ştefănel caught the little boy and, with the same switch he had used to hit the dog, he started hitting the child. But that child's mother had just returned home, he was a child with a mother. Ştefănel had no idea what that meant. The mother, like a fire-breathing dragon, ready to gobble up the entire village, rushed to the guilty boy's house. She shook Ştefănel twice and had her son hit Ştefănel with that same switch.

Probably in the exact moment when he raised the switch to hit Ştefănel, the dog died and moved inside its master. Ştefănel began to whimper like a dog and he looked at the little boy he had just beaten with the same pathetic eyes Rex had. The child got scared and started pleading with his mom: Let the dog go! Let the dog go! The grandma also yelled at her not to kill her grandson, the boy's mother went over to the dog, took the chain and pulled the dog out of the cage, dead. Ştefănel was howling slowly, the way a dog foretells someone's death. The mother got scared as well, she crossed herself, picked up her frightened child and tore off, yelling: Behind me, Satan! Behind me, Satan! She says that after that, her little boy began stuttering, he hadn't before. And Ştefănel dreams of the dog and its bone, he howls like a wolf dog, he doesn't go to school anymore, because of his aggressive tendencies. He's liable to bite any child. It seems that his grandma stayed a grandma, she didn't transform into an old female dog, as we were expecting. His mother came home after she tried talking to her son on the phone and he yelped like a puppy. At school, they said that he had become an underdeveloped child, a poor student, under-educated, malnourished, with various abnormalities, asocial, unfriendly, sadistic, with criminal tendencies, and he shouldn't be associating with us. No one played with him, 'cause his bite could kill you. It was a good thing that he lived far from us, because I would've been worried about my brothers. Then they took him to I don't know what hospital, but they didn't cure him. People said that animals get their revenge too, that you can't abuse innocent creatures without being punished. That Ştefănel had the heart of a bad dog, while Rex put up with everything and never bit anybody ever. An angel of a dog. I still feel bad even now that I wasn't able the save it. I could've gone at night, with Dan, to untie it and take it with us. After all, we knew he was torturing it. I saw that dog one time. An animal with helpless eyes. We didn't realize how skinny it was because of its fur, which hid its bones. Nor did we think it would die so quickly. While I still feel sorry for the dog even now, I see its sad and resigned eyes looking out from its cage, I don't feel sorry for Ştefănel at all. He got what he deserved. I told my brothers never to torture animals, so what happened to Ştefănel doesn't happen to them. His mother says he's been cursed and she goes around to monasteries and to old babas to cast the dog out of him, but Ştefănel has gone completely crazy and he'll die soon, he's gotten thin, he barely eats anything anymore, the kids wave bones at him and he howls like a dog. His mother left again, gone after long money, his grandma takes care of him. I don't feel sorry for him. That's what he gets. Wickedness has a limit and it should be punished.

96

The babas in our village are divided into two camps. One side claims that priests leave our village so quickly because people are apathetic, they're bad and they've got no fear of God. The other babas claim that all the priests stayed, at most, two or three years until they saved up enough money for a car, grew a belly, and then they left for other villages where people were stupider and more willing to give them money. Another priest is leaving our village right now. He's younger and more handsome than the previous priest, he has a worthy wife, and three children he sends during holidays to people's doors to announce that he's coming. He also sent his wife out to earn money. Then he thought he should teach religion class in school and educate students in the spirit of Christianity. Not for free, of course. I was really glad and imagined that we'd sit and listen to beautiful things, things that would soothe our soul. We wouldn't have tests and exams, it wouldn't be hard to learn. Grandma used to tell me such interesting things from the Bible and she said that the Father at the church told her all of them. I thought that during religion class, our priest, in a gentle voice, would tell us stories, and we'd listen with our mouths hanging open. But that's not quite what happened. At first, we enjoyed listening to him because, indeed, he was a good storyteller, but there was so much noise that soon we couldn't hear him anymore. The kids wouldn't listen to him. Because of the noise, he started having us copy out texts and learn them by heart, ones about divine punishment and the forgiveness of sins. He dreamed we'd sit well-behaved in our seats, listen to him submissively and loving, while he'd look at us as if we were a bunch of sinful monsters and demons. But we're not monsters or demons. We're just a bunch of kids who've been abandoned and punished by our parents and everyone around, and, look, now by God too, for our terrible sins. We need God's mercy more than His numerous punishments. God's mercy and comfort are like the sun's rays waking you up in the morning and, when you open your eyes, you see your mom who's touching your cheek ever so lightly and she asks you: Did mama's little chickadee wake up? And the little chickadee, coddled, shuts her eyes in hopes that it will happen all over again.

Before the end of the school year, the students in the older grades decided to put the Father's patience to the test. They shouted loudly at each other, they fought and misbehaved during religion class. The teachers from the nearby rooms would open the door, thinking that the students had been left alone without a teacher to supervise them. The kids would quiet down for a second, then they'd start making noise again. The Father would get so mad his beard would become all ruffled. He couldn't stand it any longer and he grabbed a kid by the cheeks and pinched him, he threw chalk at another one and then pulled his hair, yelling all kinds of things at him. Meanwhile, two little angels were filming everything on their phones. Then the older brother of one of them, a student at the Polytechnic university, uploaded two short videos onto the internet about: "The merciful Father in religion class." I think the priest left the village because of these kids, not because of the money. Nowadays teachers are afraid of kids, not kids of teachers. Supposedly they're not allowed to hit us anymore, because they'll be banned from teaching.

We also have a social worker in the village who asks us if we're feeling depressed and tosses pamphlets over our fence about parental care and preparing children for the problems associated with migration. As if we had to be prepared for war, as if our parents would never return and we'd always be alone, we'd grow up alone.

Mom will come back and Dad will come back and everything will be as it was before. I remember what it was like with Mom and Dad home. Mom would work in the mornings, when I'd wake up, she'd be cooking, Dad would watch TV. It seems like a long time ago, like in another life. I'm sorry that Dan doesn't remember anything, and Marcel never knew what it meant to live as a family, to have your Dad and Mom with you.

⁕

During the school year, mornings are the hardest.

Everyone's yelling that they want food. The pigs, dogs, chickens. And my brothers don't want to wake up, they don't want to wash themselves and get dressed. Dan's a big boy and he helps me with Marcel sometimes, after he's already woken up. My brothers would eat at nursery school, while I, usually, wouldn't manage to grab a bite. I'd feed all the animals, but wouldn't have time to feed myself. And, as soon as I'd get to school, all I could think about was food, if only I had eaten at least a slice of bread. And if it were a harder day, with tests, with quizzes, I couldn't make it through the final classes. I'd be about to faint of hunger. Sixth period was usually chemistry. I liked our chemistry teacher, she would explain the lesson to us clearly, without yelling at us that we're a bunch of stupid idiots, and I understood everything in that class. Sometimes I'd ask to go, because I was hungry. I'd tell her I didn't feel well, my head hurts, please, let me go home early. She called me into the chemistry lab one time: Is it that you don't feel well or that you're hungry? And she gave me some treats to eat, then I became friends with her daughter and we'd eat together in the lab. The teacher would say to me: My daughter doesn't usually have much of an appetite, but with you she eats like a wolf. She'd explain to me what all those little boxes and bottles and test tubes were for. She kept an old radio in there and she'd put on some music for us. Chemistry became my favorite subject and I became good friends with the teacher's daughter. But I didn't have time to study for the other subjects and I didn't eat in the chemistry lab every day. I told Mom that my grades aren't that good because I don't have any time to study. I come home from school and eat something, because I'm dying of hunger, then I refill the water tray for the chickens, feed the pig again, it eats three times a day, the way people do. It hears when I come home, it can sense when I'm eating and if I don't give it anything, it grunts and squeals loud enough to scare all the neighbors. Then I cook so we'll have something to eat for dinner and, if anything's left over, to have something to take to school the next day, I clean up a bit around the house or wash myself. Then it's already five thirty, I run to the nursery school, so my brothers won't be the last ones there and start crying, abandoned and forgotten. The nursery school isn't that far from us, but the teachers won't let the kids go home alone, someone has to come get them. I get both of them, and after that, with two little brothers, whiny and noisy, I have to do my homework. Sometimes I manage to, other times I don't. Mom told me not to worry, as long as I don't flunk, because anyway she's going to save up money and I'll go to college on a paid spot, I won't have to get a scholarship, wherever I want. There's no way I would flunk. I hardly study at all and get B's, imagine if I studied! The chemistry teacher also told me that I'm her best student, it's too bad that I have an entire household to worry about and I don't study enough. It's fine, this works too. Thank God we're not keeping rabbits anymore. They're such a pain! My cousins have some. The kids and parents both are constantly picking grass for their rabbits. You hardly have anywhere left to pick it, and the kids waste so much time doing that! Rabbits are very cute, how can you roast them and gulp them down after you've petted their soft fur? Now, during vacation, when the nursery school is closed for two months, same as my school, I take care of my brothers all day long and the days pass more slowly.

At night I read them books. Dan chooses the book, then Marcel wants to choose one too. We let him. He likes to come over with his own book, he wants me to open it and read to him specifically from his book. He chooses it by the cover, because he doesn't know how to read, he's still too little. Dan has learned a couple letters, but he knows what most of the books are about because he remembers them, I've read them to him before. Mom would read us books too . . . These books aren't for kids, but they insist I read them to them. When it seems to me that they've fallen asleep, I shut the book, and they both jump up: We're not asleep, read us some more, don't go. It's a good thing I have them, otherwise I'd forget the alphabet, I don't have any time left to read. Sometimes after my brothers had fallen asleep, I'd keep reading. The title of one of the books was *Viticulture*. It was probably Dad's book, because Mom would read us books that were much more interesting.

⁂

I did something bad. I mean I didn't, I mean I did.

I'm not afraid of the dark and I went outside last week around twelve o'clock to see why the dog was howling. It was howling so pitifully it was as if the dog were dying of a broken heart, from missing you two as well. Then I listened more carefully. It wasn't howling from longing or because it was dying, but from pain, in a way that you don't really hear dogs yelp. And I thought that maybe the chain was choking it, maybe it got its paw caught in something, maybe it crawled into its cage and couldn't get out anymore, or who knows what might have happened now. I went outside at night, I wasn't afraid. The dog, when it heard me, stopped crying, its eyes glimmered, transformed into two small, greenish shining lights, like the cats', but more terrifying, so that the hair on my arms stood straight up, perpendicular, it would've stood up on my head as well, if my hair had been shorter. But the dog was fine, it wasn't choking, its paw wasn't caught, it came over to me and licked my hand, wagging its tail, while I checked it. I went back inside and I slept like a log and I don't know if it howled again or not.

The next morning, a neighbor, someone's father, who had just come home for a few days, saw me sweeping through the yard and called out to me.

— Heya, Cristina (he knew my name, but I don't know his), was that your dog howling last night?

— It was ours, I don't know what's gotten into it, howling at night.

Then he came into our yard and went straight over to the dog.

— Bravo, Spot, old boy!

— Ciarlz, I corrected him.

— Ciarlitto (I'm certain the man works in Italy). Bravo.

Our dog didn't bark at him and it let this stranger pet it. And I didn't understand what he was praising our dog for.

— You celebrated Easter last night, didn't you. With some thorns along the way, your nosey wosey kind of got pricked, but you caught it. Where are the spikes?

The man picked up a black clump from the ground.

— I'm going to go throw this hedgehog skin in the trash. Do you know how many chicks and how many birds this rotten hedgehog has eaten? Because it's obviously harder to catch mice than chicks. Forest animals had better stay in the forest, otherwise they only cause trouble. I've been after it for so long . . . Maybe it has babies somewhere too and it was bringing them food. And it ate my ducklings when they were already so big! It would steal one and run away, no one could catch it. It would hide somewhere nearby and come out at night to hunt people's birds. And, look, your dog caught it. Would you look at that, bravo, doggie.

The dog seemed to understand that it was being praised and it spun around near its cage, wagging its tail.

— Mine's a good dog too, but I think its chain is shorter and it couldn't have caught it. Or maybe it had a nest right under your wood stack. It didn't eat any of your chicks?

— We don't have any chicks this year, just a couple of chickens. Mom's going to buy full-grown birds in the fall.

— As for buying, you can, but what's yours is yours. You know what you're putting in your mouth.

— Well, you struggle to raise them, only for them to be eaten by cats, or rats, or hedgehogs. One year, Uncle Colea's cat ate nine of our goslings.

— Well, yes, well said. You're a big girl. Your ma's off working. Your pa too. And you're by your lonesome with the farm. That's why you're so smart. Life teaches you everything. Even your dog is tougher than other dogs.

— I don't really feed it meat.

— Who feeds their dog meat? It got some for itself, even if it was hedgehog meat.

And the man left, carrying what was left of the hedgehog in his hand.

After about three days, I heard the dog barking again as if someone were dying. It had just gotten dark. We all went outside, Dan with his little hammer. The dog was barking and straining so hard in a certain direction that it almost broke its chain. I saw a hedgehog cut across our garden. I quickly took the hammer from Dan's hand and threw it at the hedgehog. I don't think I hit it or maybe I did just a bit with the handle of the hammer because the hedgehog stopped. We ran toward it and surrounded it, and it curled up into a ball, so that you couldn't see its head or its little paws anymore. It was small, maybe the baby of the hedgehog the dog had just eaten. It had seen that its mother wasn't coming back and it went out in search of her.

Dan brought over a metal sheet and he banged on it with his little hammer to see if the hedgehog would react, but it just flinched. The dog was happy that we had caught the hedgehog and it was dying for us to hand it over already. As if it had a right to the hedgehog. The dog had barked, it had called us over, and thanks to it, we had caught the hedgehog. The hedgehog didn't try to run away even when Dan stopped banging on the metal sheet. We didn't think then of letting it go, letting it get away. The dog was already drooling in anticipation! I pushed the hedgehog with my foot over to it. The hedgehog rolled like a ball. Ciarlz didn't want to eat it in front of us and waited for us to walk away. I warned the dog that it better not yelp that it pricked its nose, right as we'd be going to bed, not letting us sleep and waking up the whole village . . . If we hear one sound, we're coming to take the hedgehog back. And the dog didn't make a sound. The dog understands everything. Sometimes it understands even when you don't clearly tell it what to do or not to do. While you can talk to people for hours on end and they still don't understand. The next morning, we went to get the hedgehog skin, because in this heat, if it stays out for a while, it rots and attracts longish yellow flies, that carry who knows what diseases. I looked for the skin and didn't find it. There's no way the dog could've eaten the hedgehog whole, spikes and all? Maybe it buried it somewhere . . . I suddenly felt so bad for it . . . How could I have thrown an animal that little, innocent, and beautiful to the dog? At least if the dog had caught it by itself I wouldn't have felt so bad. Maybe this one had no intention of eating chicks and chickens. Hedgehogs are good and useful animals, and we threw it to the dog. We could've taken it to the edge of the forest or the other end of the street, farther away from our house and our birds. I could've let it live, because it's a living creature, too, and it has the right to live. I'm so sorry, I feel like crying. And what an example for the children, who will grow up cruel and hard-hearted . . .

✎

Dan doesn't tell me if he loves any girls, but Marcel openly admits who he likes and who he wants to marry when he grows up a bit. I'm certain that the girl Marcel is head over heels for, is, in fact, in love with Dan, who's in the same group at nursery school with her and who's the same age as her. Marcel brought her over to show her some toy and the girl played with our little tractors and toy cars, just as if she were a boy. Then they played in the sand and I saw Marcel pull her toward him, they both fell down on their butts, and he kissed her, I couldn't quite see where exactly, because they had their backs toward me. But he definitely kissed her and the girl sat there politely, waiting for Marcel to be done. Then she looked around for Dan. I was peeling potatoes on the steps, and I could see everything clear as day. Dan, the man of the house, didn't waste his time playing with snot-nosed kids in the sand, instead, he was intent on moving sticks from one spot to another, as if the sticks weren't fine where they were. I didn't criticize him or tell him what he was doing was pointless, so I wouldn't embarrass him in front of kids who were visiting, especially when they were girls, and I left him alone. And our Dan was so serious, glum, cold, and indifferent! The girl got up from the sand, she arranged her braids, smoothed her dress, and got out in front of Dan:

— Do you need any help?

Dan walked past her, carrying his sticks, he didn't say a word, not a muscle on his face moved. You'd think that this snot-nosed girl wanted Dan to kiss her too! She was the same height as Dan, cute and neat. It's a bit early for Marcel for all that kissing. But Dan can be tenderer with girls, when it comes down to it. The girl didn't allow herself to get intimated by Dan's indifference and she started carrying sticks as well. They were both carrying sticks without even looking at each other. Why didn't I think to make them sweep the yard? It would've been so clean now, with so many volunteers! Marcel was sitting like a dope in the sand, dizzy from such powerful and drawn out emotions. Not even Lucian and I kissed each other with such lengthy passion. The way this younger generation is growing up, first they kiss each other, then they learn how to walk. Dan with his pretty classmate from nursery school were carrying sticks, and I left for a second to take the potatoes inside, and when I returned, no trace of Dan, no trace of the little girl. Where did they disappear to so quickly?

When I asked Marcel, he philosophically shrugged his shoulders, like an eighty-year-old man:

— Dunno, he answered briefly, lost in thought.

He seemed to love her a lot, but wasn't at all jealous. Crina is my girlfriend, he'd repeat to everyone. And now his Crina disappeared with Dan, and they're surely already playing doctor in some hidden corner of the shed or in the attic, and Marcel doesn't even care. Dan also had other girls he played with, I caught them undressed, poking each other with sticks, supposedly they had gotten sick and were giving each other shots. Lia told me she did the same thing when she was little, when I told her I caught her sister curing Dan. And now Dan is teaching Marcel's girlfriend and so on and so on, continuing the tradition. In Lia's opinion, these are innocent children's games and I shouldn't fret. I'm worried that my brothers might end up the same as Veronica's cousin, who got inflamed too young, a stallion in heat, and in elementary school, and no one knows what to do with him. You can't say that boys go bad if they don't have a father, that one had a dad and what good was he! His dad wanted to do him a favor and took him · to women, so that the boy wouldn't grow up frustrated and so that he could learn the procedure, so no girl could deceive him. And look how that turned out! So, if you have a dad, it doesn't mean that you'll grow up to be a decent person, and if you don't have your dad with you, it doesn't mean that you'll be a hoodlum and a lowlife. My brothers won't turn out that way. I'll catch Crina and tell her never to step foot here again. She has both brothers wrapped around her finger, and plays them both.

Lia told me it's not good to raise boys without girls around, because afterward they become shy, withdrawn, and dumb. Girls are more devious and deceptive. It's enough for one to lift up her skirt and she's already making him marry her. Let them feel them up a bit, undress them, because they can't get pregnant like that, the girls like it too, otherwise they wouldn't stay there still as sheep. If you keep them on a tight leash, boys will grow up wild and afterward they'll pay for it.

But Marcel is so little, when I was his age . . .

Don't worry about it, when they're little, they like girls and shout that they love them, but when they get a bit older, they don't even want to hear about them, they don't want to see them! What, do the boys in our class look at us?

They do look, I know that Lia's got someone, though he's a year younger than her. Both their parents know about their relationship and they bought them tickets to the circus in Chişinău. Though she's pretty young, Lia wears a little silver ring. I have a thin gold chain, but I'm afraid to wear it, because some drunk might yank it off. Mom bought it for me, but Lia got her ring from her boyfriend, who carries her backpack full of books home for her and invites her out for strolls, he's teaching her how to ride a bike on the school soccer field. He's an only child, his parents are very hard working and they didn't go abroad, they work in the village and they get by, they're the best farmers in the village, they also have a small pond with fish, they're doing well. Sigh, I have too many responsibilities to waste time with boys. I have to take care of my brothers and I don't have time for love, the way other girls do.

I wash their hair once a week, Marcel is little, but Dan could wash his own hair, I make their beds every day, I wash their clothes and iron them if need be, I cook for them and set the table, then I wash the dishes, and Dan, when he's in a bad mood, calls me all kinds of names: for him I'm a goddamn woman, bowlegged beanpole (though I'm not at all bowlegged, he's the only bowlegged one), horse face, he slams the door and leaves. And Mom keeps telling me that it's no reason to be mad at him, that I should go talk to him nicely and gently, because he's a very good, well-behaved child. If I didn't have these two snot-nosed brothers, I would've been in Italy a long time ago, with my mom. I would've taken care of a child too and I would've gotten a thousand euros a month. I'm taking care of two here and what do I get for it? In Italy, I would've made a lot of money and then come home, to marry Fedoraş, or I would've stayed there, at a prestigious school for *stewardesses*. I want to work on a plane because I'm not afraid of heights, I don't get dizzy, and I can hardly wait to skydive at least once.

I told Mom as well: Marcel definitely has roundworms! He must have kissed that stray cat, or played with our dog or with scabby kids. Everyone eats, we eat too, we're growing and our bodies need food, but Marcel eats nonstop, as much as a grown man, and after just a little while, he's hungry again. It must be because of stomach worms! As for growing, I haven't really seen him grow as much as he eats, and he's not fat at all. He eats quickly and greedily, I caught him eating macaroni and cheese out of the pot. All I did was ask him: Are you full, Marcelly, or do you want me to give you some more? See, though we're bigger, I put the most on your plate!

Yes, I'm full, he said. And then he waits for us to leave the kitchen so he can go through all the food I was saving for the next day. Auntie said that's how men eat. But Dan doesn't eat that much, and it's not as if he were a girl. Marcel eats in secret, as if I wouldn't give him food if he asked. It's true that he asked a couple times at first and I didn't give it to him. He wanted cookies one time, but I had divided them up for everyone for the next few days and I told him the rest were for tomorrow morning. Once, I hid some pastries and he asked me as sweetly as possible if he and Dan could each have another small bite.

I would've given them a bite, but if I had brought them out, they would've seen the spot where I had hidden them all. And then bye bye pastries! The two of them would've eaten them all, down to the last crumb. I know it, and the next day, I'd have asked: Where are the pastries? And Marcel would've shrugged his shoulders, completely confused, good question, where could they be, and Dan would've given his opinion, some cat or dog must've eaten them . . . And both of them so serious! I know it!

❀

Everyone knows now what "yours, mine, and ours" means. Your child from a previous marriage, my child from a previous marriage, our child from our marriage now. There are more and more of these kinds of kids in our village, for example, Costică's little boy, who he had with the Giantess, after his first wife left him. She left him with two kids, two little boys, to take care of by himself, as a punishment for all that she had suffered during the time they had lived together.

Rodica was very young when she had gotten married, she had never been with another man before Costică, she had never been kissed by anyone other than him, so he had nothing to hold against her. The age gap between them was ten years. She was very delicate, thin, and beautiful. After just a few months of marriage, she had become unrecognizable. She walked around wearing an ugly old headscarf, rubber galoshes, and thick long socks, and she always had on a kind of unisex robe, the kind that workers on the tractor crew used to wear, I never saw one actually, because we don't have a tractor crew anymore, but that's what people said. She looked like a forty-year-old baba, but not even babas wear headscarves like that or galoshes, she more closely resembled a great-great-grandmother. She was very ashamed of dressing so ugly and she walked quickly on the street, her head held down, avoiding having to talk to anyone. In general, she didn't have a single friend and she didn't talk to anyone. Her husband wouldn't allow her to dress nicely. Not even as far as the well, if she dressed normally, in a T-shirt and pants, and Costică saw her, he'd begin calling her all kinds of names and take off her clothes while they were still out on the street. She'd be almost naked by the time they got to their yard, she'd run inside the house, and he would throw her clothes into the stove and set them on fire, then he'd go inside the house and beat her until she was bloody. Rodica was too ashamed to scream, she didn't want to risk the neighbors hearing or coming and seeing her completely naked and beaten up, or to complain to her parents. A younger sister of hers, one of my classmates, told us everything. After she had her first baby, she had a second one, but her husband still wouldn't leave her alone. She threw herself into a well, scratching up an elbow and her head. People got her out and they were furious with her, because she had polluted the well. The water's no good anymore if a woman has thrown herself in it, and now they have to detour around half the village, old people and sick people, carrying two heavy buckets of water from who knows where. The second time she wanted to throw herself in, a man saw her and said that rather than dying so young, it would be better for her to go off into the wide world. Because there's life beyond the borders of her yard. What had she seen at twenty years of age? Go! And, at the first chance she got, Rodica left. She never returned to our village, it's been years, she didn't come to see her children, she didn't send them money either, there was no word from her.

Her parents avoid answering questions about their daughter, they're ashamed about everything she went through without them being able to help her in any way. They had been happy to marry her off young and get rid of her.

Costică stayed with his two children like that for a bit, and then he wanted a woman. But who would give a man like that a second look? As soon as he lured anyone, the scrawniest or ugliest woman in the village, immediately a bunch of house-wives would gather at his gate, with the ugly one's mother out in front, who'd scream at him: Give me back my daughter, you criminal! Do you want to light her on fire, instead of logs? You're cold and you need fuel? There were many of them, some-times armed with axes or sticks, and Costică wouldn't argue with them. In the end, the Giantess moved in with him.

The Giantess is a nickname, because she's a tall, strong, sturdy woman, when she turns a boob of hers in your direction, you automatically shrink and tremble a bit, and if she gets mad at Costică or at someone else, she breathes fire out her nostrils and smoke comes out her ears. She had had a few husbands before, she'd beat them whenever and wherever she'd catch up with them. She'd go back home alone, then she'd return for them, she'd hoist them onto her back and carry them home. Get up, you drunk, I've carried you all my life, dragged you up after me, and I'm still picking you up from the middle of the road! Then she'd change her tone: Drunk and mean, but mine!

Costică brought her over from the neighboring village and had a child with her. He fears and respects her, from time to time he gets a beating from her. God is great, and if you do good, good things come to you, if you do evil, you receive evil. Everyone says he got what he deserved.

———

Supposedly, one time the men, as many as were left of them in the village, went to harvest hay. Everyone packed themselves something to eat, because they had to work all day. Costică had found a piece of cooked rabbit in the refrigerator. Around noon they sat down to eat, but just as they had gotten their food out, the Giantess showed up, as black as thunder:

— You took the rabbit from the children's mouth, you drunk!

And she began gathering up the people's food, she didn't stop at the rabbit, she also took some pastries, some cheese, enough for about three days, the onion was the only thing that didn't interest her. Among those men was also an Armenian who had lived in our village for many years with his Armenian wife, and he didn't accept women making fools of men.

— Crazy evil woman! he snapped at her.

Then the Giantess took off a shoe and threw it straight at the Armenian's head. She took off the other one too, offering it in the same way to Costică, and heckling him:

— Don't bother coming home unless you bring my shoes!

And she walked off, barefoot and triumphant, leaving the men hungry and humiliated in the middle of the field.

❦

I remembered how I used to stroll with Fedoraş through the village. I had barely started going to school, we were in the same class and we were already looking for a spot for our future farm and designs for our house. He dreamed of a big house in the center of the village, close to all the stores, I wanted it to be close to the ravine, close to running water where the goslings could feed in peace. We looked carefully at all the houses.

At one of the houses, we liked the gate, decorated with little bunches of grapes or storks, at another, the large windows with pretty curtains, at some, the yards were so clean that you could eat off the ground.

Then Fedoraş left for Italy with his parents and he's going to school there now. Mom didn't tell me what city they're in. But I know that, one day, Fedoraş will come back and marry me. He loves me a lot. I'm waiting for him to finish school. He'll come and we'll build a house in our village, the most beautiful village in the world. And if everyone leaves and the village becomes deserted, we'll have many, many kids and fill the village back up. Our children will take over the abandoned houses, they'll grow up big and strong, they'll work and the village will flourish.

%

Veronica is a girl who's gone bad, she's just three years older than me, but she seems much older because she has big breasts, she's tall, and fat. She doesn't have a dad, her mom works abroad but doesn't really send her enough money and no one takes care of her. At first, she lived with her grandma, then she moved into her own house, meaning her mother's house, so she could be a whore without anyone bothering her. Her grandma had three daughters: the oldest had gone to Russia, to Tyumen, and had gotten married there, she has two kids who speak Russian, the middle daughter married a tractor driver from our village, the youngest daughter was unlucky, she got pregnant while still unmarried and never got married afterward.

I remember Felicia Petrovna, Veronica's mother, the village librarian, the most beautiful woman in the village! Thanks to her, the entire village, especially the men and children, would often visit the village library. We were happy even to catch a glimpse of her just walking down the street. She'd go to work with her hair pulled back, she had big dark eyes, very white skin, and lips that looked just like Angelina Jolie's. Veronica isn't as beautiful as she is. We'd go to the library to see her smile at us, we'd take out a book and return it the next day. She'd ask us: You finished reading it already? A book that thick? Yes, we'd answer. Well tell me, how does it end? We felt sorry for her when she was sad. We knew she was unhappy, alone, that she was unlucky in love and things didn't work out with her and men. People said that she didn't even need a man. Because she was better off without having to worry about some drunk and, whenever she needed anything, all the men jumped to help her. They'd fight among themselves, who would till her soil, who would harvest her fruit. She had inherited a little house from her grandmother, and modernized it a bit, fixed it up. She didn't need that much to live on, she had a job in these difficult times, when those who have only land are left without crops and without any income in years of drought, she had a little daughter who was a comfort to her, her older and richer sisters would help her, as would all the men of the village. The women would say that people were so attracted to her it was as if she carried around honey. A younger child had heard his mother saying that Felicia has honey and he asked her one day: Where's your honey, ma'am? I would've thought that it was a made-up story, except that when I was little, I had also heard that she carried honey, only I felt I knew where she kept her honey: between her breasts, in a teeny tiny bottle, wrapped up in white lace. And I imagined how, whenever Miss Felicia would walk more quickly, the honey would trickle out from the little bottle, everyone who touched her would get stuck to her, exactly the way they did in that story, when whoever touched the fool Ivanuska remained stuck to him, and he arrived in the city of the eternally pouty and weepy princess with a long train of people behind him and made her burst into laughter. For this, the king gave him her hand in marriage. I imagined Miss Felicia, with her puffy dresses, walking victoriously down the street with scores of infatuated men sticking to her like flies, unable to escape. Felicia had a house, money, a child, but she didn't have a husband. That was the explanation for her leaving.

The problem was that her daughter was left home alone with a dirty uncle who could hardly wait for her to blossom. What's more, his wife, meaning Felicia's sister, wasn't home either, but had also gone after long money, leaving him alone with their two sons. And she'd send him money, either to repair their fence, meaning that instead of their wooden fence, which wasn't in fashion anymore, to get one made of concrete with little flowers, the kind farmers have now, then to switch out the furniture in the house, to build another barn for the sacks of grain and corn, and so on. The man works around the house, he doesn't make any money, because no one needs his broken down tractor. He took care of the vineyard, so he'd have something to drink all year long. Sometimes his wife's money was spent on who knows what, meaning whores. They say that the uncle went over to his niece's rather often. Now many girls avoid Veronica, because she's gone completely bad . . . She says her mom doesn't love her. If she had, she would've taken her with her, she wouldn't have left her alone with all the drunks . . .

I spoke on the phone with Lucian, who asked me nicely not to talk to Veronica anymore, not to play with her, not to have her over.

— Please! he insisted over the phone.

— You've been to her too! There's a reason your mother won't let you stay in the village.

And I was so angry I felt like crying. So he's a man with Veronica, and with me he pretended to be a baby.

⁕

There was a circus yesterday in the neighborhood next to the school. We went too. Mister Andrei beat Missus Agripina again. He kept beating her until the ambulance came. We had stayed this time too, until we had gotten hungry, but the ambulance hadn't come yet. At first you could hear the screams and blows. We couldn't hear them from our house but Ghiță called us. Come on, hurry up, he's beating her again. When we reached their fence, about twenty kids had already gathered there. Some had climbed up onto the fence, others were looking through the slats. I, since I was taller, could see over the fence if I stood on my tiptoes a bit. Actually, there wasn't much to see. He had already chased her around the house, he had snapped at the kids who were gawking, scaring them with the axe he swung threateningly toward them. She had baked bread that day, so she was tired, she was puffing like a whale, she already had a heart condition, and he had caught her quickly. Before catching up with her, he had thrown the axe and this time, apparently, he had hit her, in her elbow or her hand, so he wounded her, and when he saw the blood, he was struck by his great love for her. We, too, saw the wall that had been splattered with just a little bit of blood. At least we saw that much. If we hadn't known where to look, we wouldn't have even noticed it was there. Missus Agripina was lying passed out behind the house, behind the shed, resting after all that running. Only a couple people went in to see what the situation was and to comfort mister Andrei who was crying really hard.

He thought, as always, that he had killed her and that, finally, he would go to jail. Agripina would always say: Maybe I'll die by your hand and you'll end up in jail, you fascist!

We caught the moment at the end.

Now, like every other time, the man fell to his knees, and ripping his raggedy shirt and pulling his hair, he bellowed as loudly as he could: Agripinaaaa, I love you! Agripina, I can't live without you, my precious little wife. I've wronged you, forgive me, my beloved wife.

It would make us all melt with delight, he'd say that to her so beautifully, it was as if he were reciting one of Mihai Eminescu's poems! And he'd say all kinds of sweet things to her until the ambulance arrived. We'd hear everything, because he yelled really loudly, so everyone would hear how much he loved her. And he kept getting redder and sweatier. Given that she was passed out, we don't know if she heard. The neighborhood women would tell her afterward, to please her. But she didn't believe it. The most exciting moment would be when the ambulance would arrive. Then it seemed he'd really go berserk. They had to have two or three stronger men who could hold him back. The whole village could hear when they'd start fighting and the women would go in search of sturdier men, knowing what would follow. The men would have to hold him back tightly, because otherwise he'd throw himself across the stretcher, he'd grab onto the ambulance door and, in general, get in the way of the doctors giving the woman first aid or taking her to the hospital.

Because of his heart-rending wails, the babas and the other women in the village nicknamed him "The Mourner." They said that with music and verses like that, he'd earn a lot of money at funerals, because now there are hardly any more wailers left.

— He's still rather young to be a wailer, one man said.

— It'll upset the dead if this one wails for them, another man said. He's kind of a lecher, and his wife, if she makes it out alive this time, will die by his hand next time.

In fact, everyone was expecting for her to die. Two or three times a year, for several years in a row now, an ambulance comes and gets her, though they say that a person can't survive more than three heart attacks, Agripina still hasn't died. The doctors have gotten bored too, and look, they're not coming anymore. She's black-and-blue, almost dead, but after a few days, she comes back home, her bruises heal, nothing hurts her anymore, she becomes the same nag she was before. And again she begins pestering her man that he doesn't have any money, he doesn't have a fence, he hasn't finished the house, he didn't harvest the hay on time and it got moldy, what will the sheep eat this winter, that the sparrows ate their sunflower seeds, that he didn't get in good with the right person and he didn't get elected even assistant mayor. That you spent all the money again, you cheating sonafabitch. That everyone saw him with that whore who's been with everyone in the village and the county, and you probably got all kinds of diseases from her, you've infected me, you beast! And she keeps going on like that, the biggest nag in the entire village. And when he beats her, the village weeps for him, the fine one, the fiery one, he again couldn't stand all that torture. They cry for her only when she's out cold, when she doesn't say a word, doesn't reproach him for anything anymore. Then the women say: She was always running off at the mouth, but she didn't deserve to be killed. With her weak heart, she could die if someone even yelled at her a bit louder, let alone if she were made to run, chased and threatened by a drunk husband, throwing his axe at her . . .

⅔

The mothers are coming!

Just as in the children's story about the goats, the mothers are coming home, trembling from fear and anxiety, will they find their kids waiting for them at home, or did the wolf eat them? The children cry when their mothers, who are timid and shocked by how much their babies have grown in their absence, return. The mothers of the children in the village have come home because, right now, they're on summer vacation, our mother is the only one who doesn't come.

It doesn't even cross my mind that I'd want my grandma to die and that way Mom and Dad would both come home immediately. That's what all grandma's children decided on and that's why we're home alone this summer. Our parents decided not to come twice and spend money on tickets. Last summer Dad came home for a couple of days and did some work, fixed some things up. Then Mom came home on vacation. But this year they're waiting for grandma to die first.

Mom, when she cries, doesn't cry in front of us, she says, hey, I have to organize some things in the shed or the pig is yelling for food or she finds some other excuse to hide herself, and then, after she's had her fill of crying, she comes to us smiling. And Marcel, who Mom had barely gotten to hold in her arms, when Mom comes and she's busy with the suitcases, with phone calls, he wants to stay close to her so much that he curls up tightly around her leg. Mom doesn't say anything, she lets him, she'd like to hold him, but she can't now, she doesn't have time. She walks, or rather she drags herself around, with Marcel still clinging to her leg.

And once, a while ago, Marcel hid, I don't know if something had scared him, but we all kept calling to him: Marcel, Mom came home, Mom's looking for you, and he was hiding under the pillows in the parlor. We started to pull him out, but he held onto the pillows and screamed, he screamed even when Mom held him, as if her arms were too hot and they were burning him. Now he doesn't hide anymore. Mom brings him clothing, toys, cookies, and beautifully wrapped chocolates, and he waits as impatiently as we do.

We take turns talking on the phone, in order of age, from oldest to youngest. Mom asks me what I've been cooking and if we have enough food stored up to eat, if we're feeling okay, if anyone's hit us or called us names, if any relative has brought us something good to eat, if we have clean clothes, if the washing machine, refrigerator, television are still working, if the house is tidy.

Then it's Dan's turn, and he tells her what toys or clothes he'd like Mom to buy him next, who hit him (if that happened), and he always tells Mom that something somewhere hurts and Mom says to him: Put the receiver there, where it hurts, and Mama will kiss it and make it better. And Mom does a big kiss into the receiver, there, does it hurt anymore? Dan: A bit, and Mom kisses it again, until all of Dan's imaginary boo-boos are better. I know there's nothing wrong with Dan, he just wants attention, Mom would kiss him some more, but Marcel is waiting too.

I don't know what Marcel talks about with Mom, I mean what Mom says to Marcel. We only hear her begin with: How is mama's little chickadee doing . . . She doesn't call me mama's little chickadee, her pet name for Dan is "mama's young man" or "the man of the house," and Dan almost steps on tiptoes to be taller than me when she calls him that. He walks around the yard like a tough guy for three days afterward . . .

Marcel, who knows how to say everything and talks nonstop, so that you sometimes snap at him: Hey, be quiet, motormouth, doesn't say anything on the phone other than mama mama mama. All his vocabulary is reduced to this word, which he speaks in all different tones, as if he were singing, and we walk away, so we won't burst into tears.

Once Mom came home and Dad called: Hey, what's wrong, are those tears of joy that your ma came home? Then in a sadder voice: I can sense that my cubs are crying. Dad never calls us chickadees, only cubs. He also calls us super cubs, like the kind in fairy tales, and sometimes he calls me daddy's helpful pretty girl.

My beauty isn't exactly blinding, but Mom showed me some photos of me when I was two in which I was very cute, look how pretty you were, when you grow up, you'll be just as pretty and the boys will be dying over you. Right now you're still growing, you're more angular. I'm waiting to be grown-up, round and pretty.

I'm afraid that Dad will come home this time without a tooth in his mouth, same as Petrică's dad. That's how people who work in northern Russia come back. Not all of them, just the greediest ones. They mine precious jewels that are full of radiation and that makes their teeth fall out. If it weren't dangerous, they wouldn't allow Moldovans to work there, to throw money at them. Last time, Dad seemed older when he came home, thinner, and he was missing two bottom teeth. It didn't look very good, I didn't say anything, but Marcel asked him to put his teeth back in, because he's so ugly it's scaring him. Dad got sad, he promised that he'll get teeth put in next time. I felt so sorry for him. It's for us that he stays there, far off and alone, slaving away.

℀

We celebrated Dan's birthday. Six years old! Next year he'll start school. I invited all our cousins, plus the two boys Dan likes, his friends. I also invited the teacher's daughter, Alina, who I like. She brought us a big cake and a ball. Our aunts brought us food, because Mom asked them to. We bought a cake from the store, we didn't know we'd receive another one. Marcel picked out a toy, which he later didn't want to give to Dan as a present, he said it was his. I asked him nicely: Give it to him just for tonight, and tomorrow you'll play with it again. Dan will receive lots of toys, he'll let you play with it. And Marcel gave him the present. All the kids came with gifts, except they were mostly kitchen towels and little cups, not toys. Because their parents don't have money to spend on gifts, so they gave them what they could find around the house.

I put the entire cake from the store on the table. I didn't put all of the cake we received from the teacher on the table, just some of it, a few small slices, I put the rest in the refrigerator, so it would last us a couple days. I put a tablecloth on the table, the white one, and a child spilled a glass of compote on it and stained it. I put pretty candles on the cake and Dan blew them out, and Uncle took pictures so he could send them to Mom over the internet. We don't have internet yet, people in the village are just starting to connect to it, we don't even have a computer. Mom said she's going to buy us a computer and we'll learn how to send letters through the internet, and we'll talk to and see our parents. Mom will show us the new gifts she's bought for us, and we'll stand in front of the screen and she'll see us. Meaning she won't miss us so much, and we won't miss her so much either, if we see each other all the time on the screen.

When Mom brings us clothes, we put them on and go out on the street, we circle the neighborhood, we go to the store, then to the well at the end of the street, where some woman asks us: Did your ma bring you clothes from Italy? Then she says: Well, well, don't you all look nice, I hope the evil eye stays away.

Mom, when she comes, asks us what mama's darlings would like to eat. We, all three of us, say different foods and she makes everything each of us said. Marcel wanted an egg. I said to him: You dummy, you eat eggs even when Mom's not home, I make them for you. Mom's are better. I didn't get mad. Mom makes us a ton of food, which she puts into small bags and sticks in the freezer. After she leaves, we take them out, one by one.

Sometimes she washes things in the house, sometimes she hoes the garden, if it's summer. Mom works so much when she comes home that I think she's able to catch her breath only back in Italy, even though there's a lot of work to do there too, according to her.

⁂

These men go away to make money, leaving their women home alone, with the entire farm on their shoulders. The wife tills, the wife plants seeds, the wife picks the fruit, the wife cuts down the hay . . . And how can a woman get by on her own? She finds helpers. And some men, most of them alone as well, aren't looking for money when they help, but women. Angelica from the end of the street, whose husband has left, has taken up with a guy, who does all her work. But to bring in wood from the forest, you need two men, to load it into the cart. After she had brought the two of them home and served them generously, they didn't know how to share her. They fought, they beat each other up, and word was that one died from a powerful blow. Now the talk in the village is that, since the man was drunk, it's more likely that he fainted and wasn't dead, a strong man doesn't die just like that. The other two got scared, what should they do with the body? They cut it into bits, they filled two buckets with cut-up man and emptied them into the outhouse at the back of the garden.

Their neighbor, Missus Olga, was convinced that Angela was stealing her geese and eating them with the men who'd come over. That evening, she heard noise at her neighbor's and thought: That whore, she's having a party again and feasting on my geese, that I struggle to raise and keep like the apple of my eye, so I have something to send my children! When the noise had died down at Angela's, Olga went in search of her geese. It seemed like everyone was asleep there and she could freely inspect the place. She went in, saw blood on the ground. Aha, I caught her this time! she exclaimed, triumphantly, and she followed the traces of blood to the outhouse. So, she gobbles up the meat, but she throws the guts and the down in the toilet! When she took a closer look, peeking up from the hole, instead of the supposed bird guts, she saw the hands, feet, and head of a man. Stiff fingers. She almost died of fright on the spot! Even now she goes around to hospitals searching for a cure.

When the police came to take the two lovebirds away, Angelica, drunk and cheerful, yelled after the village policeman: Kiss kiss, brother-in-law! She was on good terms with all the men of the village, including this actual relative of hers—our police officer was a very good-looking man who often stopped by her place. This expression of affection on the part of a murderer, in front of his boss, didn't sit too well with the police officer. After that, they assigned a different police officer to our village.

❀

A few years ago, humanitarian aid was sent to our school and each box contained a "Kinder," meaning a chocolate egg with a small toy inside. But someone had opened up the boxes and stolen the best things out of them. My box, for instance, was missing an egg. I thought that *kinder* meant egg. Then a child from somewhere else told us that it meant "child" and he taught us the kinderland game, which involved the younger kids playing with the older ones.

The more kids that participated, the more interesting the game was. At school, during our long recess, we'd each choose a role. Most of us stayed students. A single kid played the role of all the teachers, meaning that very few teachers were left at school and the couple still there would teach us all the subjects. We'd form a semicircle around the blackboard on which he'd write out the lesson. The child-teacher would come into the classroom, bent over, limping, and smoking a colored crayon. He'd cough the cough of a chronic grouch, imitating our teacher, and write "French Class" on the blackboard, then yell as loudly as he could: BON JOUR! and look down at our feet. We could barely keep from laughing now, but, at first, when our actual French teacher had yelled at us, we had startled and gotten scared. He, pleased, started to look under our desks: Did anyone dribble? At that time, I didn't understand what he meant. Only after a few lessons did we realize that he was expecting that we, because of his bellowing, would wet our pants and he was looking under the desks to see who had peed. Did anyone dribble? our classmate would ask and stare at one of us and say: You, you dressed up cow! Go to the blackboard. Other than *bonjour*, our teacher never said anything else to us in French. He, in fact, isn't even a French teacher . . . The kid sent to the blackboard would erase "French" and write "Romanian." The face of the child-teacher would change, to our great delight, and become all sweetness and he'd make eyes, with slightly lowered lids, at the girls whose chests were growing. During Romanian class, the nouns "chest," "waist," and "blouse" can't be declined without the teacher groping their form, number, and concrete case: And by the time you tell your dad, you dumb cow, you'll have flunked and be in school forever! You're in seventh grade and you barely know how to write, you clueless sheep! To my great relief, he didn't grope me, because my chest hasn't grown yet and we have so many chesty girls in class! And they say that next year a new young teacher is coming. Lord, have mercy and send us a new teacher, preferably a female teacher, and save us from this scourge, who doesn't teach us anything anyway! Then a girl would come in and play the role, one at a time, of the other teachers. Next was "Geography." Obama wants to renovate the White House and he asks his councilors who the best construction workers in the world are: The Moldovans, siiir Obama. Some of the buildings they've repaired or even built are the Eiffel Tower, the Dubai airport, Petronas Towers in Kuala Lumpur, Two International Finance Center in Hong Kong, the Empire State Building in New York, Hagia Sophia in Istanbul, the Sydney Opera House in Australia . . .

Wow, Obama says, very impressed, and where do these Moldovans come from?

(Here, a kid, one of Obama's councilors, has to show him where Moldova is on the map.) — A country this little has such great construction workers?

No, siiir Obama, Moldova is their office, they're everywhere in the world.

The geography teacher gave us homework to draw a map of our village and to write the names of the countries where the villagers have gone to on the map. Everyone from the neighborhood or just our parents and relatives. Then, during class, we'd each tell her what we knew and she'd write all the countries on the board. From our village, the only place no one's gone to is Africa. Yet.

Then we play police. A boy with a belly (he stuffs his hat or a jacket in his shirt to look fatter) plays the role of the police officer. Two people on a farm catch a robber who had just been trying to steal their pig. We're gonna tell the police officer on you. They go and tell the police officer everything. Yes, we'll take care of it, we'll set things right. You go home, he tells them. The police officer goes to the crook's house: So you tried to steal the pig from off the people's farm. Seven years jail time . . . or, I need some help too, I'm building a house and I need some people to work on it, I've already got a couple other guys just like you, but I want it completely finished in a month. It would be a pity for you to go to jail for seven years for a pig you weren't even capable of stealing. And I'll see to those people.

And another police scenario, one we love: a man is selling grain and bran cheaper than at the market and he's doing well. There's a line outside his gate, the man is making a lot of money. The police officer comes by, he sees he's doing well, but you could use some security, you need protection. The man says he isn't that rich and what robbers live in our village? So he doesn't need anyone. And then the police officer goes to the robber, his friend, and says to him: Hey, go over to that guy one night and mix his grain and bran a little, so he knows whether or not he needs our protection. No sooner said than done. And that man never sold anything anymore and he never got richer, because he didn't want to split the money with the police officer.

Yes, kinderland is our favorite game. We play it after class, in the evening, during vacations. The little kinderland, the big kinderland. The one we laugh about and the one we cry about. We also play hide-and-seek, tag, red rover, we jump rope, we build things in the sandbox.

With my brothers, we play Mom, Dad, and baby. A kind of family kinderland. I'm the mom, usually, Dan's the dad, and Marcel, the baby. Lately, though, Marcel doesn't want to be the baby anymore, he wants to be the dad, but Dan won't let him, so Marcel's the mom, and I'm the baby. I cry very nicely as a baby, and I say: Me want milkie, me want bottle, and Marcel melts with delight. I've said it before that Marcel should've been a girl! I let his hair, which grows into ringlets, get long. First it turns up at the tips, like a duckling's, then it gets all curly. Mom says we all had ringlets when we were little, then our hair straightened out.

When we cut Marcel's hair, it was pure drama! Dad, when he had come home, had said to him:

— Marcel, you're a big boy, and it's hot outside, let's cut your ringlets a bit, so you can be like us men.

He agreed to it, he sat quietly on the chair, and Dad cut his hair. But when we brought him a mirror and he saw himself, he started bawling:

— Put my hair back! I want my hair back!

So for now I'm letting him keep his hair long, we'll see about it later.

❧

A village all our own must exist somewhere, one with its own laws, with a way of life that's inaccessible and hidden to others. Where life carries on beautifully, generously, compassionately, without meanness, longing, and waiting. A village of good children. Notice I said "good." Not just a village of children, that already exists. Every village in Moldova is a village of children, the entire country . . . Especially if we count the old people, who have also become childish. Normal, healthy men and women, capable of working, who live in the village are a rarity, a minority. The children's Moldova. That sounds really nice. We're building a bright future for our children. Yes, except that we're building it in Spain, Italy, Russia, because we've already built everything in the Czech Republic and they don't need any more construction workers. Spain, actually, is in an economic crisis. Kids with parents in Spain were happy about that. Crisis—a magic word, which means parents will come home, to their kids. But none of them came back.

⁹⁶

My new friend's name is Alisa. Her mom is from Ukraine and her dad is Moldovan. Her parents work in different countries, she's lived more with her grandmothers. Her grandma from our village does witchcraft. They say that Alisa is learning by watching her. At first, I didn't even know her name, everyone called her the Witch. She's a bit taller than me, she has blond hair and light colored eyes, she says they're gray now, but they were once blue, then green, and when she becomes a woman, they'll change again. They're her transitional eyes. She doesn't have any other close friends besides me. She's been to our village before, but I've gotten to know her better only this summer. She came to our house with a pail of summer apples and called to me at the gate. She also had a jump rope with her and we played together a bit. Then she told me a secret. That she's a witch and she can teach me to be one too. First, I have to learn how to stare the way she does, I'm not able to yet, I have a lot to learn. Alisa told me that witches have eyes that can make others afraid. Come closer and look at me. I came closer and looked straight into her eyes. Her eyes got bigger and bigger, and then they started shining. I got scared, I screamed and ran away, and then I calmed down. I like Alisa a lot.

Though she hasn't spent much time in our village, because she usually lives with her mom, Alisa knows all the crossroads, all the magical or terrifying places, all the dried-up and abandoned wells, the hole the nymph is chained up inside, waiting to be freed, the little path that ends at the former den of a bear or another very big animal, the fork in the road where singing is heard at night, she knows all the old baba witches in our village, friends or enemies of her grandma. She said that our village is blessed with gentle creatures, for whose sake the rest of us are tolerated. And that for now we don't have monsters in our village. I don't believe in these kinds of stories.

I thought that Alisa speaks Ukrainian, but even at home with her mom she speaks our language, and she knows only a little Ukrainian, she's learning it only now. The thing she'd like most is knowing all the languages people speak and she has lots of little books from which she studies all the languages of the world. And during the fall she has a private teacher in her village, but she also goes into the city on Saturdays, to learn more foreign languages. She tells me words in her different languages, which I forget.

Alisa knows where there's living water and where there's dead water in our village. Every village has living water and dead water, she didn't learn about that from the fairytale by Ion Creangă, but from her grandma, who's old now and can't wander through forests or on hills in search of springs anymore, so Alisa has gone over all the forests and hills. In the morning, while the dew's still out, without eating, clean, you have to wash yourself really well, her grandma gives her an herbal bath with different plants, then she blesses her, and sends her out in search of springs. May no one bite you and no wild villain come upon you to tempt you. And Alisa was protected from dangers and she found healing water. It really does help you sleep well and it's good for healing wounds, stomach problems, blisters, and other things. Dead water keeps for longer and it stinks of rotten eggs, living water is good only until the next day, but you can't tell others about the spring so they don't pollute it. I can't tell you where it is. You have to find it yourself.

She brought me plants to make into a little pillow for sleeping at night, for tea that should be taken in the morning or the evening, for my brothers' scrapes, for protection against the evil eye, pain, and the surrounding wickedness, for softening and taming wild animals or people, for the well-being of our household. And two pebbles for Mom and Dad, so that they'd be healthy and nothing bad would happen to them, and for them to come home quicker.

Alisa said it's better if you share what you know with people. She also came over in the evening, when my tired brothers were going to bed. She got close to my brothers and rubbed their ears and shoulders, so that they'd sleep better, and said that I should massage them at night too. They lay there as still as cats, they didn't move a muscle. Then the two of us stayed up and talked and I found out all kinds of secrets from her grandma, who had allowed her to share them with me.

She said that for people like us, who understand the nature of things, life will be hard. Not everyone can learn the art of healing and you have to agree to take on difficult things. It's a sin not to help people, especially since it's so simple sometimes, so little is needed, sometimes even just squeezing someone's hand can heal something. And she squeezed my hand in many ways. See? Yes, there are bad witches as well. They have the same amount of power as the good ones. But the largest group by far are those who don't care about anything and are untouched by any spell, who are just taking up space on earth.

She told me you can live every day as if you were on holiday, feeling like you're floating or shining with joy. But not now, only after you accumulate good deeds. The more good you do—not only to people, but to all creatures, in general, you can take care of a little tree, it's still a good deed—the more soul you accumulate. Do you know that there are people who can really float? They have so much soul that it lifts them off the ground.

Alisa talks a lot and I listen to her without ever getting tired. We make all kinds of plans, we write all kinds of spells for situations that come up in daily life, she teaches me all kinds of magic touches for improving health or fulfilling wishes. We eat the summer apples she brought me. Our family doesn't grow any, few people in our village have apples like these. Her grandma sent her to bring us some. Our neighbors have already picked theirs and they don't have a single apple left, but in any case, they weren't as sweet and juicy as these are. Alisa will leave soon. It seems as if, even though we haven't seen each other that often, I've known her for a lifetime, and each of our visits has been so full of stories, events, trips, miracles, everything around her is so intense, it's as if she had stayed a year in our village. She sometimes plays with some of the neighbors' girls, who I know too, but late at night, carrying apples, she visits only me. And only us two invent magic games. And when she leaves, I'll stay and crack an egg at the crossroads from time to time, and pour out a glass of water for the abandoned nymph, and wait for the bear in front of its den . . . I want to transform into a nature girl, like her. I want my eye color to change and my eyes to shine too.

Alisa called her dad and he came. She cast spells for him to come with flowers and herbs, she put out pebbles, lifted spells, and thought about him a lot. She had barely gotten to know him at all before she was already big. Her grandma loved her and Alisa would come to our village to visit her, but her dad was never home. Always working abroad. If she was able to call him and he came, I can call my parents home too.

I learned that the place of troubles is a space that's half enclosed, with deep walls, hidden, remote, abandoned, forgotten by everyone, damp, overrun with weeds and moss. It's also called the place of fears and you come here to rid yourself of lesser fears, pain and sickness, sadness and disappointments, especially those caused by love.

— The place of meetings is the best place to go when you have wishes you want to be fulfilled. You find this place at crossroads, lots of people pass by there, they meet, they cross paths, they don't leave their dread here, but their joys. It makes people happy when they meet. Not neighbors they're fighting with, but people they haven't seen in a long time. Even if it doesn't make them happy, they say hello, study each other, look at and smell each other, the way animals do. The street is a social institution. Even if they can't stand each other, a husband and wife don't fight on the street where people can see them, they dress nicely, they eat before heading out, they're calm. The message they're sending to others is one of health, well-being: Everything's going well for me, I look and feel good. The crossroads is the place of beautiful thoughts and it's best at twelve o'clock, day or night. But you have to not see a soul in any of the four directions of the road. No one can be on the road, exactly at twelve, and you have to spin around nine times, in the middle of the crossroads, with your hands in . . .

— And the egg?

— The egg stays in your pocket.

She had said that the first time you touch the egg you're sacrificing, you put it on your chest, between your breasts, on your stomach, over your belly button, and you keep your eyes closed. And you put a spell on it. If you go to the crossroads at night, before that, at twelve during the day, the egg has to look at the sun, not long, so it doesn't go bad. If you go to the crossroads during the day, you leave it out at twelve at night, to look at the moon. That is, you leave it out during the night because nothing will happen to it, it won't go bad, nighttime is cool. You first grab the egg with your left hand, you'll want to take it fresh from your own roost, not from the roost of someone else, who's touched it with who knows what thoughts. After that it doesn't matter what hand you hold it in, what matters is that you break it using your left hand as well, at the crossroads, you lift it up three times, this way, in your hand, and the third time, you smash it against the ground. It's better if you pick up the shells so that no one comes along and takes them and steals your wish. What would someone who sees eggshells in the middle of the road think? They'd immediately think that there's something unclean about that. You pick up the shells and bury them the way you bury impossibility, and possibility remains in the middle of the road with lots of people passing by, they're all going somewhere and they arrive at their destination. The same way people reach where they're going, may your wish arrive safely, may no one stop it. Shells are the thick parts that remain on the ground when a bird emerges from an egg and flies away. A chick hatches from an egg by breaking the shell. In the same way, may your mother fly at the thought of coming home, may she be overcome with longing for her children. In the same way, may your mother arrive home before the chick hatches from the egg.

But the hardest thing is to order your thinking, Alisa had said. A wish is a thought. You might not believe it, but sickness is also a thought, even people, as a whole, are a bunch of thoughts. Dressed in flesh and bones, and clothes.

Good thoughts and bad thoughts are the same distance away from us, they both envelop us. If people would let only good thoughts win, the world would look different. But many people can't defend themselves against bad thoughts, and others even search them out, they need them. Evil is just as nourishing as goodness, people who rejoice at evil feel as satisfied as good people.

Evil isn't always the opposite of goodness. We, kids, don't understand that. Nothingness is their opposite, nothingness is a kind of politeness, apathy, indifference. Evil is alive and it's closer to goodness than indifference. It's like love and hate, which are only one step away from each other. Evil is a state with feelings like regret, remorse. Indifference is a state of deadness, without any feelings. It's hard to fight against it.

Thoughts have to be educated, disciplined. Especially when you take a thought to the crossroads. Your thought has to travel a long way, it has a lot of work to do, and sometimes a lot of fighting to do. Your thought has to be clean. Any other smaller idea, hidden, forgotten, drags it to ground and prevents it from reaching its destination.

— My thought is for Mom to come home. A very short thought: Mom home!
— Then go with it, with this thought, to the crossroads

at night. Italy isn't that far away, if you fly in a plane, but thoughts aren't made of steel, a thought passes through thousands of other similar thoughts, because all kids dream of their mothers coming home and they ask them in their thoughts to come back and then the thoughts get mixed up. The mothers get mixed up and who knows whose mother will be called by your thought and which happy child will enjoy his mother's return. Or the thought is too weak and it dries up along the way, or it gets there without any real strength, the mother cries for three minute over her babies left at home, then she dries her tears with the edge of her sleeve or with a disposable tissue and continues working there among strangers. Also, the thought shouldn't be sent to the heart, but to the head. At the heart it will lead to a few tears and that's it. It has to be felt by the head, so it thinks rationally about whether perhaps what she's gaining isn't worth what she's losing, whether being with her family and children isn't better than living alone far away, with strangers.

For the wish to be fulfilled, you break the egg, you leave the yolk in the middle of the road, but that's not enough, you have to send your thought and wish, the egg isn't transformed into a bird that will deliver your thought. You offer something important to this place, and it will offer you something just as important. If you want to receive something, you also have to give something. You'll notice that even when you find something, either you had lost something before and now you're getting it back in a way, or you'll lose something afterward, something just as precious. What you want from the crossroads is the energy of the people who have passed by there and have arrived where they wanted to go. The egg has what the crossroads doesn't, life is born from the egg, the egg has everything and it doesn't need anything. It is the center of all things. You believe, symbolically, that the crossroads needs this element and you offer the egg to it. I don't know if the crossroads really needs something like that. Maybe not. But you have nothing better to offer. I think that crossroads have miraculous powers even when people don't go by there that often or meet others there. I've gone down roads like that through the forest and they've charged me up with power. But I'm a nature person, even the trees offer me their warmth and strength. And you're still a civilized person, you know how to read only a few people around you, a few signs from animals. You don't even know that if you want to understand a person better and get along better with them, you have to start with little creatures, to understand smaller animals, plants, first. They're simpler, clearer, kinder. And they're so gentle that you can fill up your heart enough for an entire lifetime.

People ask for so much gentleness, they ask for love and sacrifices, without offering anything in return, as if they deserved everything. But it's not right, because the more you want, the more you have to be prepared to offer. People who don't understand this, who don't know how to respond to every gift, they don't love and they don't respond tenderly, become stupider than animals. They're a waste of space on this beautiful earth, as Grandma would say. They waste the treasures of this world that are given to them abundantly. They just sleep, eat, and poop. And they cover over everything with concrete. The earth shouldn't offer these people anything. They completely ignore crossroads and magical places and they always want to dominate. And these rebellious places exist, unexpected spaces, where power gurgles up, it teems, gushes out, communicates, gives, asks for, fights against, takes revenge, plays, inspires awe, horror . . . And mankind wakes up and finds that it's smaller and weaker than an ant . . .

— Besides the places I told you about earlier, there's another kind of place, which you have to find by yourself, your soul has to guide your feet toward it. Sometimes you come across it without knowing. Inexplicably, you feel good there and you want to stay a while longer, to catch your breath a little. This is the place of happiness. You feel light there, you forget all your worries, you forget everything, your memory disappears, your hunger and all your needs disappear, nothing moves, time has stopped flowing and you feel complete peace all around you. And you surrender to that state, in which your body and soul are one with the nature surrounding you. I know several places like that, but I can't tell you where they are, they're mine alone. There are lots of them in this village, it's a big-hearted village, alive and generous.

— I think I have a place like that. I call it the island. A place where I lie on the grass and look at the sky. When I'm there, I don't miss my parents, I'm not hungry, I'm not scared, even though I'm alone. Even after I leave that place it's a long time before I get hungry or miss anything or want anything. There, at the edge of the forest, in the abandoned orchard near our vineyard, is the place I visit every year. The first time I discovered it, I was little, my parents were working in the vineyard and I went to look for walnuts. I went in and everything stopped, maybe I disappeared in that circle of earth. My parents noticed I was missing and they were looking for me everywhere, they got scared, where had their little girl disappeared to, and I was close to them, but I didn't hear anything and I was watching the clouds through the branches of the walnut tree. It was as if I had entered another world, as if I were practicing for heaven.

I was lying in the grass and the bugs, butterflies, and little flies were landing on me and tickling me. When I got up and left that place, I was so happy it felt as if it were my birthday, and I had received many many toys and gifts, Mom and Dad were kissing and hugging me, and I had also eaten an Eskimo ice cream bar, made in Bălți, and everything in a matter of seconds and all at once, all those pleasures combined. As if I had woken up from a very happy dream. Then I didn't go back there for a long time, and when I returned, I was afraid that the miracle wouldn't happen again, that it had lost its charm and was now like any other place. I would find it quickly each time, by its grass, the shade of the tree, and the ground seemed a bit higher there, like the tiniest little hill. And, each time, I lie in the grass and wait for nothing to happen, I tell myself, it was all an illusion of mine, I had fallen asleep and dreamed a place like this, an island like this, but slowly slowly everything starts up again, the very gentle fluffy clouds, the bugs that tickle me shyly and pleasantly, the soothing grass, and the sensation that all the possible joys and pleasures in the world are gathered together here, and they overwhelm you all at once, and you can hardly stand so much love, pleasure, and peace. Then everything slowly, slowly pulls back, returns to normal, the sky is the sky, the grass is the grass. And for a long time I feel this full, almost heavy beauty in my chest.

— Yes, that's what it's like. I feel the same way. I had gotten signs that the two of us could be kindred spirits. Maybe you're the fairy of insects or tame clouds, I knew that you had the mark of flowers on you. Grandma told me that too. Maybe you'll receive other signs as well.

༄

Any kind of running water can be living water. But in our village living and holy water is the water into which the church's icons were thrown. Our church is very old, its icons had been brought from far away, from Russian monasteries. People from all the neighboring villages would come to our church to see them and pray. Then new leaders came in, with new people and new laws, and they closed down the church. After a while, they thought, why should a place that could be useful for the community be closed? The directors went in, they tore out the icons, they took the carpets. They kept the carpets, but if they had kept the icons or one of the holy books, they would have been fired from their jobs. They could have let the villagers take them and keep them, but they didn't want to. They went at night, in secret, into the forest and threw them away. People still search for them in the little streams that crisscross the forest.

Only once did someone, a girl who later became Alisa's grandmother, find a splinter on which was drawn a hand with elongated fingers. Alisa's grandmother showed the splinter to the old people in the village and they recognized it as a fragment of one of the church's icons. It made the people very sad. They had been looking for icons in the river, they hadn't known that before the icons were thrown in, they had been ruthlessly chopped up. How could you find pieces of icons after all these years? From then on, Alisa's grandmother started healing sick people and animals. They say that the splinter with the long fingers, which she found in the stream, helps her do it. Meanwhile, the bosses who destroyed the icons are just fine, they haven't been struck down by any divine curse. Everything's going extremely well for them, their children, and their grandchildren. For now.

I don't know if it's true, but long after that regime and the people in power changed, they say that two delegates came to our school building during elections one summer to campaign for some party. One of them was tall and thin, the other was shorter and fat. The new outhouse had just been built and people likened the old outhouse to a romantic ruin but, in fact, the spot that grass had recently grown over was a dangerous swamp you could drown in. The two delegates fell in there, and when the tall one yelled Help! Help! trying to get out of the swamp, the short one screamed at him: Don't make waves! Don't make waves!

Now the old outhouse is used only for the butt-kissing of true friendship. When two kids declare themselves to be friends, they go to the abandoned outhouse and kiss each other on the butt. I don't know where this tradition comes from . . . I don't think our moms and dads did that.

When I was in first grade, all we had was that old outhouse and it already looked like something out of a horror movie. It had countless holes everywhere. The roof had caved in, due to shoddy construction. When it rained, it dripped everywhere inside the outhouse. The walls had big holes in them because the people nearby, when they needed stones, would come and break off pieces of the wall, being careful to take out the stones in such a way that the outhouse didn't completely collapse. After all, it's the school's toilet, it belongs to all our children. When you walked in, the weaker slats on the floor had fallen into the stinky hole that was almost full. Our clothes would reek for an entire day after going in there. The little kids from the lower grades would burst into tears and go back, some had been there only once in their life and that had been enough for them. Once inside, most kids would pee out of fear, not just because they had to go. The walls dividing the girls' and boys' sections also had holes in them and the boys would watch the girls and then tell everyone what kind of underwear the girls had on, what color or what kind. The boys smoked there without fear of getting caught. Teachers never went in there, even now I can't imagine a teacher peeing. The outhouse gave you the feeling that every bad spirit had gathered there and was watching you, that all the witches were inside hiding behind the corners. When you had an enemy, you wished with all your heart that they'd fall into that place. But I personally don't know anyone who ever fell in besides the principal's daughter. She was a beautiful girl with long golden hair, and when she fell into the toilet, the older boys pulled her out by the hair so she wouldn't drown in the filth. The girl was my age then, now she's graduated high school and has started college. She had stunk so badly and the kids wouldn't stop laughing! Only after that did the principal order that a new, civilized outhouse be built. After we started using the new out-house, the old one remained as it was, it took about two years for that swamp to dry up and harden, and then become overrun with weeds. After it dried up, it didn't smell bad anymore, people kept stealing the stones but something resembling the former construction remained. The outhouse even had half a roof, and some pieces of its walls were still standing. Kids today maybe don't even know that it was, in fact, the school outhouse. Now we go there rarely, about five or six of us classmates, filled with nostalgia and regret that time is passing so quickly, that even the school is getting old. No one remembers the stories and the things that happened in this place anymore, surrounded by trees and tall grass as it is now. No one knows for sure if the swamp has completely dried out, or whether, if you were to fall into that hole, some hideous toilet nymph wouldn't drag you down to the bottom. When you think that our mothers had used the same toilet, except that in their time it was new and clean, without the tiniest hole in its walls . . . I'm still expecting to run into some spirit or a witch when I visit that outhouse. And I'm not the only one. All the kids are expecting that. We thought that something was haunting it, it's a place that always gives rise to an inexplicable fear.

I went there one summer, when we swore true friendship, for life. Terrified, we kissed each other on the butt, as a sign of total loyalty. Usually, boys and girls kiss each other. I don't think I've heard of a girl kissing a girl. I kissed Fedoraş on one of his butt cheeks, and he did the same to mine. We were tanned but our butts were white, like little kids who still drink from a baby bottle. Fedoraş felt from the tone of my voice when I said: Your butt's so white! that he had disappointed me. I hadn't realized that he was so young. He answered: It'll get darker as I get older. As if he weren't man enough with butt cheeks that white. Mine were just as white, but he didn't say anything. We weren't afraid only of spirits, ghosts, the dark, the wind that was whistling through the walls, but also of the kids who might catch us taking our underwear off. We looked around, terrified by all kinds of rustlings, we quickly kissed, no one had seen us. After this ritual, we got over our fear. That happened a long time ago, when Mom and Dad were at home, and I was Fedoraş's girlfriend.

Years later, when Alisa the witch came to our village, I rediscovered the place. Without her, I never would have stepped there again. She taught us unbinding spells there. She said that unbinding spells can be taught only in magical places, like this one, and at a magical hour, the middle of the night. If Mom had been home, she wouldn't have allowed me to go out by myself in the middle of the night. So I got to learn some unbinding spells, but I haven't used them yet. These words carry a certain weight and you shouldn't say them unless it's necessary. If you say them just like that, whenever you want, the way you would a poem, or you tell someone who has asked to hear what an unbinding spell sounds like, then these words will lose their power. We spun around the outhouse, so we could gather strength. Alisa said this place isn't an outhouse anymore, it's a place of troubles. I didn't understand why and she explained it to us: intense feelings and thoughts have been stored up here, fears, secret thoughts and desires, forbidden ones.

People have left their excrement here, all that's bad in them, so this is a place of evil.

She said I was wrong. Children have gathered here, hundreds of kids, thousands of times, and child caca is sometimes even healing for adults and old people. But that's of no interest to us. Kids were afraid here, they came to meet fear. When you get frightened, you lose energy. Kids produce more energy really quickly, but the energy that was lost stayed and got stored up in this place. Can't you feel it when you enter? You don't feel it during the day, because the sun is powerful and fear is afraid of light, that's why you can feel the energy of frights only during the night. It can also be bad, but that depends on you.

— No one learns everything only from schoolbooks. You also learn from birds, animals, from the earth, and from your body.

The ones who teach themselves are powerful. Eyes can look inside as well, not just outside.

Every person has a little marble, a little sphere, in their chest. In some people, it's cloudy and heavy, in others, it's light and see through. The sphere is shiny inside people who are happy. As if someone had polished it. The marble represents the harmony of things, peace and being reconciled to yourself and what surrounds you. It shines brighter in kids who are young and innocent, and in wise old people. In bad people, the marble darkens and then gets smaller and smaller, until it melts away and disappears. Those people become either like robots or like wild animals, without reason and without a soul. In order for little ones not to lose their sphere, they have to be loved, they have to be hugged lovingly. For grown-ups the rule changes. If you're a grown-up and someone hugs you, it's not a bad thing, but it's not enough. You also have to give love, not just receive it.

Our witch also says the devil doesn't exist. That he's made up. It seems to us that the outhouse is a diabolical place. She says that it isn't, that places like that don't exist, that certain people can be diabolical, but not places. What exists are places that are hidden, chosen, full of energy, magical. She believes there's only one kind of energy and each person is responsible for what they do with it. There are weak elements and strong elements, meaning weak people and strong people. In places like these, they can either create or destroy. They can raise themselves up or fall down. Strength is needed whether you're climbing or descending. Your legs hurt both when you walk up too many steps and when you go down them. A powerful person isn't someone who has simply been handed everything, money, fortune, influence, because you won't be given that all the time throughout your life, maybe you'll receive something once or a couple times. A powerful person is someone who knows how to obtain energy and strength from their own heart, the person who energizes themselves, builds their own hydroelectric plant. Which produces light from the inside. There are very few of these people. Actually, all people have their own hydroelectric plant, but they prefer to get their light from the government. They don't realize what a source of light their own being is, what wealth they have inside them. People are walking treasures, there's a reason why the other creatures submit and bow down to them. There's something superhuman about people. They're witches.

— Like you?

— No, much more bewitching. But they don't know, they don't realize, their eyes and hearts are blindfolded. And they die like that, without seeing their marble light up. They don't even know how to look at the sun anymore. They don't see how much beauty is in them and around them.

Our light can also be lit by the sun, the supreme energy. Sickness and sadness wouldn't exist if we received from the sun everything it's offering us. After all, the sun is like free medicine without an expiration date, you just have to know how much to take and how to take it.

Alisa speaks more and more quietly, until her voice becomes a whisper. At night, in the deserted and rundown outhouse, it seems to us that we can see in the dark because of the light of our bodies. We finally scatter, each to our own house, and we aren't afraid of anything.

I feel the marble in my chest sway as I walk, warming up my chest.

———

We went to those places often, sometimes there were more of us kids and we made lots of noise as we played. We'd jump over fires, race each other to see who could climb the tallest tree, and play hide and seek. We hadn't been afraid of anything, until a car full of hunters scared us and then we didn't feel like playing noisy games in the forest anymore. The hunters said we'd scare even the frogs away the way we were screaming like we were possessed. There were both girls and boys there, all of us from the older classes. The hunters caught a girl and asked her if she had seen the boar. When she heard about a boar, the girl went quiet. Until then she had been screaming, as if she were half kebab, though hunters don't catch young girls in the forest to roast them over a slow fire. I don't think anyone had heard about a boar before then. It terrified all of us that a giant, aggressive, and dangerous boar was roaming around our forest.

Whoever helps us catch it will receive a present. What would you like? A cell phone so you can talk to your ma?

Lots of people in our village already have cell phones and an internet cable has been laid. There's internet at the school, the town hall, and the medical clinic. If there are enough kids in school, at least seventeen in each class, and our school isn't shut down, we'll win a grant and we'll have computers in each classroom. But by the time that happens, I think I'll already have finished school. Maybe at least Dan and Marcel will be there for that. Of the kids there, not one of us had a cell phone and we all dreamed of owning something like that. After the hunters left, we gathered around the girl and asked her for more details. A boy from our village remembered a story. He's the son of a woodsman and he had heard from his father that they had brought a wild pig to Bălți that turned out to be very tame, they say it would eat out of your hand. I don't think it's true, a colt will eat out of your hand, not a pig. Try feeding our farm pig out of your hand and you'll see that your hand and the apple in your hand are all the same to it. Let alone a wild boar brought over to be hunted! But maybe it was too gentle for the hardened hunters' taste. Then they decided to release it into a grove, to make it a bit wilder, so it could get used to the forest after its long and tiring journey, having been brought over from Poland by truck. Then they could really hunt it. The boar had been brought over for some big wigs and it had to put on a bona fide show. They released the boar and off it went. When they wanted to hunt it, it was nowhere to be found. And they've been searching all the forests for it ever since.

Moldova doesn't have a lot of boars in its forests, actually, it doesn't have any boars, so if anyone sees one, it must be the one that escaped. Several teams are constantly searching for it. Moldova doesn't have many forests left either. The place where we now play, where we roll ourselves into the ravine as fast as we can, used to be a forest. And now it's just grass and flowers. The houses were built at the edge of the forest, which reached right up to the village. Now the forest is getting farther away from us and it's smaller and smaller. The hunters had seen signs that the boar had reached our forest, the woodsmen were also notified so that they could find the animal's hiding place more quickly. The girl who had spoken with those people believed that they weren't even real hunters, but crooks. All of Moldova knows about this boar and is looking for it. It's worth a fortune.

We won't give them the boar! we decided. We can live just fine without their cell phone! We gathered all the kids and promised, one by one, gave our word of honor, and swore on our lives, that if any of us sees the boar, we won't tell anyone. I don't know why, but I, too, was positive that the boar had to be in our forest.

Don't walk by yourselves in the forest and, if you see the boar, quickly climb up a tree, the grown-ups cautioned us. It must be very hungry, so it definitely would also eat kids. After that incident, I really wanted to see the boar. I dreamed about saving it from the hunters and feeding it acorns from my hand. I'd be playing with kids in the meadow at the edge of the forest and then I'd go in alone, to see whether I was afraid or not, I'd walk a long ways toward the heart of the forest, then I'd go back to the meadow. Sometimes the kids didn't even notice I was missing, other times they had gone home to eat and I didn't find anyone left there.

Then Alisa came and gave me her nature lessons. She would say, we're nature's children, our parents gave birth to us and then they abandoned us. We're learning how to live and take care of ourselves alone. We get the love we need from whoever is near us and gives it to us. And nature gives us everything, we just have to learn how to receive it. It offers us more than our parents.

In the afternoons, we search for dead water. There are about three of those little streams in the forest, and next to them there has to be a big hidden puddle full of plants and tiny flowers. A place where, when you get there, a thought inside you has to whisper: Here's dead water. You have to have a small cut, or a scrape, that you splash with the enchanted water and it's immediately better, the cut and the pain, as if it had only seemed to you that it hurt. All traces of pain have to disappear miraculously. I found some swampy puddles, with stinky water, but my cuts and scrapes weren't healed by the touch of their water.

This time, a bee had stung me and the pain shot through me so fast that I teared up. I had wanted to pick a very ripe apricot, and it was full of wasps or bees that had made a small hole in the apricot and were sucking up the syrupy fruit. I grabbed the fruit without seeing them and I felt such a stinging pain that I couldn't even tell what part of me hurt. It was as if a hundred bees had stung my entire body, through my flesh all the way to my heart. I let out only a short scream, then I saw a red dot on my finger, but my finger wasn't that swollen. I stuck my finger in water and went off to the forest to find a cure. Despite the pain, I didn't forget to take a little bottle with me. By thinking of these things, I was able to keep from breaking down in tears, though I was in so much pain I could barely hold them back. If someone had seen me, they wouldn't have let me go off into the forest, alone and stung by a bee. But you can't find dead water without the help of your pain. I knew a path to the forest that cut through the vineyards and I got to the forest quickly. I saw a poplar tree with flowers growing around it. There weren't that many flowers left in the forest. Neither wild garlic, violets, hollowroot, nor pansies. It was already the beginning of July, the heatwaves had started, but all around the poplar—itty-bitty flowers. I heard water babbling close by, so there was a brook, I stepped in mud. I walked around the poplar, because my heart told me I'd find something here.

The place looked really familiar to me. I had been there not too long ago. I sat down next to the brook. I had sat here with Lucian, very close to each other! Next to this brook. I looked around and I saw a kind burrow or hollow filled with water in the trunk of what used to be a large tree. Big and small leaves, of all colors, were floating there, as if they were trying to hide the water. I stuck my finger in it and all my pain, and the redness, and the mark where the wasp had stung me immediately went away. I found it! Once you take the water, you have to wait at least a year to come back a second time, no sooner. You have to take as little as possible, to leave some for others and so the place doesn't dry up because of you, or lose its healing power. You have to make sure the water doesn't get mad and stops healing you. I took half a little bottle, for my brothers who are always getting scraped and scratched, for Alisa and her grandmother. Then I put the leaves back and I said thank you very much to the water for healing me. I was so happy that I had completely forgotten about the boar. I had found my first enchanted water. Living water is easier to find, in fact, all running water is living, you can make it healing with unbinding spells and inner purity, but dead water is very hard to find. You drink living water, you put dead water on wounds. I had all kinds of recipes from Alisa. I thought about how happy she would be and how she would study my water with her miraculous powers.

I was walking very fast, and when I saw the animal in the middle of the path, at first, I thought it was a man who was bent over. Maybe he was feeling sick and needed help, and I had just found healing water. When it turned toward me and stopped, I also froze. I couldn't move anymore. The boar was a few hundred feet in front of me. It was so beautiful, so big, so black, that I wasn't that afraid of it. But my head was buzzing with thoughts. I felt that it didn't know what to do either. After all, we were too close to one another for me to climb up a tree and, anyway, I didn't see any trees nearby, I thought about that more theoretically, just in case. We both stood there without moving, me with the little bottle of dead water in my hand, it, alert and thoughtful. I expected it to have more initiative. Then it looked like it was coming toward me. Mr. Boar, I said to him in my mind, if you eat me, who will take care of my brothers? I'm all they have! And then, I don't think I'm that tasty. Just a bundle of bones. I began to howl slowly, so the boar would think I was an inedible young wolf. It liked how I was howling, it stood there solemnly and listened, and it seemed to me that I was standing in front of a fantastical, unreal boar, that it was all an enchantment and it wasn't actually happening to me. Then I said to him, also in my mind, I'm not a hunter, I don't have a gun and I mean you no harm. Then I sang Pooooooor little turtle dove, it can't stay below, and it can't stay aboooooove. And then I went quiet because I didn't know the rest. I felt so bad that I didn't know a single song, not one! Mom knows so many beautiful songs and she asked me: What do you kids sing? We only listen to songs in English, that we often don't understand a word of, we just hum the melody. I kept quiet, I didn't move at all, I couldn't. As if I were a plant that had grown up in the middle of the road. The boar turned its head toward the other side of the path and crossed it, but very slowly, without any hurry at all, as if indifferent toward me. As if I weren't even there. I watched it, fascinated. I had never seen anything like it. Alone, in the forest. Wild pigs in the middle of the path. Only after the boar disappeared among the trees did I move one of the fingers I was using to hold the little bottle, then I took a step, then I felt a fear that back then I didn't have time to explain. A cautious step, in case the boar was watching me from behind a bush, ready to attack. It must have been dying of hunger. I looked at the trees. Not one was suitable in the event of such a danger, maybe farther on along the path there might be some branchier ones that you could climb up. Here, they were all thin and their branches wouldn't be strong enough. I stepped on something sharp and pricked my foot. When I looked down, I saw that I had stepped on a thorny twig and I was bleeding a bit. It didn't hurt, but wild animals are drawn to blood sacrifices. I felt the strength of a thousand people descend on me, and once I took off, I didn't stop until I reached the edge of the forest. I didn't lose the dead water while running and I put just a couple drops on the scratch, because it wasn't bleeding that badly. I immediately felt better. Who knows what kind of wood that hollow was made from and what kind of plants were floating in it, but the water had proven to be truly healing.

I hadn't looked back at all while I was running, but maybe, actually, not a single beast had me in mind for dinner. And wild boars eat acorns, our forest is full of acorns, why would it have needed me! I was sorry that I hadn't told the pig something interesting. Maybe it would've understood. Maybe it would've let me get close to it. Maybe I would've even given it an acorn to eat out of my hand. Maybe it was sick, something was hurting it, and I should've healed it with my water. It could find the place on its own, I had left enough of the healing water for it. At home, I cast an unbinding spell for my brothers with dead water and with wild boar which gores all scrapes, sicknesses, shivers, and destroys them, it breaks them apart with its hooves, it stamps on them, makes them crumble, drives them off, for my brothers to remain ruddy and blond, handsome and healthy, clean and full of light.

I later went down the path where I had seen the boar, carrying lots of acorns in my skirt, I called it, I reached the poplar with the hollow, at Lucian's brook. Mr. Boar, come back, please!

I'm not afraid of you anymore. But it didn't come. I hope that the hunters didn't catch it and it's still alive, roaming the forests and showing itself to good-hearted children. I didn't tell anyone. But another child, a little boy, also saw it. One who hasn't started school yet, they call him Lamby. He hadn't been with us when the hunters came and no one believed him, they laughed at him when he said he had seen the boar. And because no one had seen the beast, they had all forgotten the incident and they didn't believe Lamby. But he had seen the boar, he described it and it looked exactly like mine. Lamby said that he had wanted to ride it, he asked it, may I climb on your back, and the wild pig had nodded its head yes. Lamby had gotten close, but there was a rustling sound, the pig turned around and left. It went away slowly, it wasn't hurrying anywhere and it wasn't afraid. It was black and big. It had a hump on its back, a kind of little ridge, unlike our pigs. The kids laughed at him. But I knew that Lamby was the new Prince from the Horizon, who we, the green girls, would dance around this year. All that was left was finding his princess. Even now when I go into the forest, I think of the boar. I'm sure we'll meet again. I think about the difference between an animal that's kept in a cage, at home or at the zoo, and one that's free. The wild pig makes you think of majesty and strength, and the lazy pig on our farm inspires contempt or disgust. That one was a pig you could fall in love with. One I could've ridden on toward a fairy tale.

❦

Little Gavriliță, the chosen child, was very gentle, kids would pinch, bite, or hit him, he would scream and cry from the pain and humiliation, but if you asked him afterward to bring you an apple or let you play with his toy, he always did it right away, with tears still in his eyes. He was as gentle as a little lamb and that's why he had been nicknamed, for good reason, "Lamby."

You had to draw a big circle with his blood, and a little circle with his bones, in which a woman child would dance at night. She'd dance until blood flowed from her. The twelve girls would have to throw stones at her, but not kill her, so the holy sacrifice wouldn't be mixed with the unclean one. She had to be let go. And whoever swallowed the eye of the chosen child would bear an angel eye in her belly and would be the Princess from the Horizon. She would see the secrets of the Earth. That was just a story. My hair stood on end just from hearing it. I told it to the teacher's daughter who got so scared by the scenario that she stole the little boy away and hid him so that Alisa couldn't eat him. When his father looked for him, we told him that babas had stolen him to cast spells on him, because since he's as gentle and pretty as a girl, they wanted to turn his little cock into a little pussy. Man, when his dad cracked his whip once, we saw sparks fly everywhere and we raced to get his son, crossing ourselves and cursing the whole way. We brought Gavriliță back, who was still just as gentle, and we asked him: Are you the Prince? And he answered: Yes. Can you find your princess on your own? He didn't say anything and bowed his head. Want us to help you? Yes.

His dad calmed down when he saw him, we told him we had been joking, that we're creating an ensemble to sing and dance for the village's saint's day, when all the parents will come, Gavriliță's mom will come home from Spain, and so will lots of our mothers. We'll sing beautifully and they'll be happy at what nice, hardworking, beautiful, and talented children they have. And we're rehearsing right now, we'll make sure no one beats up Gavriliţă. And that no one turns his little cock into a little pussy.

Alisa found the place. We cleaned up and picked the plants. Each girl from the village had to come with a different kind of plant. Girls from the city or other villages, who are here visiting their cousins, could bring fruit that's ripe, and they had to be sweet. Twelve older girls and twelve younger girls, none of them could be women. The dancing woman whose blood would flow would be Veronica. We picked up sticks for the fire and brought a vat for boiling the herbs. I picked the poisonous plant, the one no one picks, no one plants, no one eats. But I know how to ask even the mandrake to be good and not crazy, to give to us and not to take, to light our way and to warm us, not to darken our path and freeze us. About four girls weren't from here, they were cousins from other places. Two girls brought little bouquets of pretty flowers, not healing weeds. Alisa said it was fine, it was as it should be. A little girl wearing a jumper dress brought the kind of roses you make jam from, not very pretty, but very fragrant. The little girl, in addition to her beautiful jumper with blue polka dots, also had blond braids and was wearing white socks. And she was the youngest, perfect for Gavriliţă. I suspected that she would be the chosen one. We danced around the fire, then around the vat, then around Veronica, then around Gavriliţă, then he and his princess were joined together and we spun around them many, many times. Veronica had been dancing only a little while when her blood started trickling on the ground. We didn't throw stones at her. She was wearing a short nightgown and she twisted like a snake, stared like a fox, and scratched the air like an eagle, and we stamped our feet so she could hear the rhythm and dance more wildly. After that, Veronica left, she wasn't allowed to see what would happen next, because she was unclean. The rest of us weren't unclean. Alisa was a year older than me, but she hadn't gotten her period yet either.

We sent Gavriliță into the forest alone. Then he came back and spun around, stepping over Veronica's blood, he smelled the steam and chose the jumper. His princess was a city girl, she was white and delicate, well-kept and quiet. She didn't say no when we took off her pretty clothes and undressed her like a doll. We undressed the little boy afterward and laid them down on the grass against each other. Then we washed them with the enchanted water, then with grass, then with water again. I remembered when I was Fedoraș's princess. We didn't have a vat with fragrant plants then, nor blood, now times are harder and it takes more effort. They laid me down on the soccer field, Fedoraș was obedient and submissive, the same as Gavriliță. He got on top of me and we stayed like that, without moving, stuck to one another, for an eternity. The green girls, about ten of them, solemn, frowning, formed a circle around us and froze. The only one among them that I knew was an older cousin of mine, who had invited me to the ritual. They had known that Fedoraș would choose me. From on the ground, in the grass, they seemed impossibly tall to me, though, judging by the age of my cousin who is now a college student, they were also girls, about eleven or twelve years old. Were they expecting a miracle to happen? How did the ritual end back then? I think someone passed by there and they thought the gathering seemed suspicious and they probably asked: What's going on over there? The girls probably got scared, they quickly got us dressed and sent us home. I can't remember the end. I walked by there many times, the grass was dried up, the soccer field seemed abandoned. I looked for the spot where I laid naked, hugging a little boy. Maybe the girls were expecting me to give birth then and there, as they watched? That's what happened a long, long time ago. Now we cleanse two children stained by unclean blood and we purify the earth, and wish it fruit and rain, because big heatwaves are coming, we pray to be protected from droughts, plagues, for our parents to come home, so there will be people to have new kids and take care of the old ones, who are still little. And for our land to remain as blessed by God as always, to have seeds and fruit, and for it not to lose its goodness.

The little girl left first, the sun was setting beautifully and slowly, as if it, too, were enjoying our ritual and were waiting to see how it would end. Then we put clothes back on the little boy and we told him to catch up with the girl, to take her by the hand, to walk her to her gate, for both of them to eat our sweet fruit on the way. Gavriliţă was very solemn and did exactly as we said. The water had gotten cold and we put the vat back onto a low fire. The first girl got undressed and we put her into the vat. She had long hair and her hair could catch fire. The rest of us were rather big for the vat, we could barely fit inside. We undressed one by one and got into the warm, fragrant water. After that, we got dressed one at a time, we each took a piece of fruit, and left. Alisa was the last one, and I waited for her. We took the vat, put out the fire, and left some fruit for the forest dwellers who don't often get to eat these sweet treats, so they'd be happy that we had come onto their territory. We each took a piece of fruit for ourselves, and scattered the rest through the grass. We took the vat to Alisa's house. It was a magic vat, used by her grandma. It was very big, but the two of us carried it easily. Her grandmother was waiting for us and she gave each of us an apple, then she gave me more in a basket so I could take some to my brothers as well, and she also put in something wrapped up. At home I saw it was some of that tasty sweet bread, with walnuts, the kind we'd eat at our grandma's, when she was healthy, at Easter.

♆

Waiting is like a small animal, neither domestic nor wild. Sometimes it's well-behaved or asleep, sometimes it's bad or on the loose, and it gets the better of reason and calming thoughts.

We only have a little bit longer to wait. This little bit is hard to bear, to endure, to suffer. It's so heavy that it drags us down to the ground and we walk hunched over from longing. Our mom wouldn't even be able to understand it. But me, when I see my brothers looking at photos of our parents, I feel a load of tears in my belly, which, if I let them flow, would drown the entire village.

My waiting is like a bouquet of giant flowers, bigger than me, sweet smelling, colorful, gathered from all our hills, which I bring to my mother, but my mother's not home. I walk in and yell: Mom! But no one answers. Wildflowers scattered throughout the entire house, on all the clean, freshly swept carpets woven in Ungheni. A tender and resigned waiting.

Dan's waiting is like a mischievous ball that's been kicked into every nook, it's flattened the vegetables in the neighbor's garden, it was caught by someone's dog who had tried to dig its teeth into it but couldn't. A youthful waiting that doesn't give up and doesn't get tired. An angry and impatient waiting.

———

Marcel's waiting is like milk that's boiling over, it won't fit into the pot anymore and spills onto the stove. Like black clouds that appear unexpectedly, they cover the entire sky and it quickly starts raining. Like an invasion of starlings or locusts in a wheat field that leaves nothing behind. A hungry and adamant waiting, with no right of appeal.

Our waiting, like a smoldering illness, a persistent virus, which only gets better when our parents are here. Dan got over his fever and cough when Mom came home. I had been afraid we'd catch it from him, but we didn't, neither I nor Marcelly. It's enough for our parents to come home for us to be healed on the spot, of all our sicknesses. Waiting is like rain after drought. We're a bunch of withered kids, dried out by longing. Like a riverbed without water. We've gotten old from waiting so responsibly and maturely, and we become kids again when Mom comes home.

A few days ago, Marcel took his little chair and set it on the front porch facing the gate, he sat down with his hands on his knees, the way they do at nursery school, and he started to wait. But it can take a month for Mom and Dad to come, maybe even more, it depends on when Grandma dies. A cartoon's on TV, let's watch, Dan urges. Look at this rosy apricot, see how it fits in the trailer of your toy tractor, and we bring it to Marcel, look how much fun we're having playing with your toy cars! But Marcel doesn't hear us, doesn't see us, it's as if he and his chair have grown roots there on the porch, he looks off into the horizon with lost eyes, and all around him springs up a world that we can't access.

When I was little, I dreamed of reaching the horizon. I would climb up the stairs and look at the edge of the earth, in the direction it could still be seen. In the other directions, everything was blocked by trees and tall fences. Around us were houses, but somewhere, in the distance, I could see green hills, yellow hills, then hills that were bluer and bluer, until they merged into the sky. At the horizon, someone had planted three walnut trees and that was my point of reference. When you got closer to the horizon, you didn't realize how close you were to the edge of the world. You'd climb the hill and that was it, you'd pass over to the other side without feeling a thing. But the walnut trees were there as a sign that you had reached the place you'd dreamed of.

Dad came closer to me. At first, he didn't say anything, he wanted to guess where exactly I was looking, he looked in the same direction as me but he didn't see anything.

— What are you looking at?

I was looking at the horizon, but I told him I was looking at the three walnut trees. That I'd like to sit in their shade one day. Back then, I hadn't started going to school yet, it was summer and I'd start first grade only in the fall.

— Well, we have a wheat field near those walnut trees, on some land we inherited from my grandparents. We can go one Sunday, just don't cry that your feet hurt. It's a bit far, a half-day's walk.

— No, I won't cry. Take me with you, please.

Dad told me the hills were different colors on account of the crops, the plants that were growing there. The forest and grass are green, corn, as it's growing, becomes dark green, but now, in the summer, it's already turning yellow, and wheat is yellow, earth that's been plowed is black or dark brown. The farther away it is, the more like the color of the sky the earth becomes.

I didn't ask him why the walnut trees were so blue.

— Look, do you see what color our walnut tree here at the gate is and what color those three walnut trees you're looking at are?

Those are more beautiful, because they're blue. Oftentimes, things that are farther away seem more beautiful, but the closer you get to them, the more ordinary they become.

But the three walnut trees guard the edge of the world, they're like soldiers.

They have stony walnuts, all three of them, and it's very hard to crack open their fruit. By the time you've gotten to the meat, your eyes are popping out from the strain. But sometimes it's worth it. A stony walnut tastes good even after five years. These trees don't produce many walnuts but they're very large.

To reach the horizon, we woke up earlier that morning, we washed our faces and we ate a lot. I ate two slices of buttered bread, an egg, and Dad spread jam on another slice of bread for me.

— Eat this too, because we have a long road ahead of us.

Mom put bread and cheese, and a bottle of water, in our backpack. She also put in an onion for Dad, he said that when you eat an onion out in the fields, it has less of a bite, it's tenderer and sweeter. And if you eat it on a hilltop, it's healthier, you won't catch cold all year long.

We walked pretty slowly until the outskirts of the village, to let our stomachs do their work in peace. We left the closely crowded houses behind, the air became thinner, and around us we could hear the music of bumblebees and the birds of the plains. We had left the village and in front of us were hills and more hills, and the three walnut trees at the horizon.

We crossed the major road, which was paved, on which cars travel toward Chişinău, Bălţi, Orhei, toward all the cities in Moldova. We crossed the small river which had dried up a long time ago. Dad had never seen it with water either. There was water in it during the war, but during the famine it dried up. People had drained the water in order to catch the fish and that's how it stayed, it's a river in name only now. It even has a few small footbridges.

We passed by the shepherd's hut and Dad asked if our sheep and goats were behaving themselves and giving enough milk. They give as much as the other animals. The goats are kind of bad. Rowdy, headstrong, if you don't run after them all day, you'll find that they've gone right into people's cornfields. I won't be taking in goats next year, 'cause it's too much work. Dad asked when it would be our turn for cheese. The shepherd calculated, in about two weeks, and the milk will be fatter then, because the heat will pretty much dry out the grass. The sheep and goats are milked every day and their milk is divided among their owners. The dog that had been savagely barking at us calmed down, and after I pet its soft fur, it rolled on the ground and put its paws up.

— Your girl has a good heart, the shepherd said. My dog can tell, it's been guarding sheep since it was just a puppy.

Dad said goodbye and we continued on our way. I asked Dad if sheep had good hearts too, Dad laughed. A dog that watches over sheep is smarter than one that's been kept on a chain all its life, and you can trust it when it barks at an enemy or fawns over a good person.

Then we crossed the big river. We walked over the bridge with the colorful trash. The big river didn't have much water in it, it hadn't completely dried out, but Dad said that in a couple years at most this would be just a gully, the same as with the small river. People leave their trash under the bridge, sometimes robbers gather there and cut up a sheep stolen from the sheepfold or a man that's an enemy of theirs. The bridge hasn't collapsed and it seems well-made. The water will dry up, but the bridge will remain there, unmoved. It was built during Soviet times, when stone was stone, and brick was brick. Now everything's imitation, it's flimsy, cheap, and it quickly falls apart, it doesn't hold for long. Now people draw stones and bricks on houses and walls, but before, they really were made from stone and brick. A car drove by and got us all dusty. It raised up a gray cloud behind it.

Then we reached the village pond, it's in a valley and can't be seen from our porch. I couldn't see the walnut trees from by the pond. Dad said they'll appear as we climb. Only about three more hills and we're there. No one was fishing in the pond. No one was swimming. Before, there was always a ruckus going on. The pond had a whirlpool and even some of the best swimmers would drown there every three or four years. Now someone had bought the pond and everything was off limits. He guards it with a rifle. Dad found a small stone and threw it in such a way that it jumped very nicely a couple times in the water, splash-splash. He gave me a stone too, I threw it without a splash-splash, but it made lots of waves. There was plenty of water in the pond and it was clear. I saw a little frog, but no fish. Dad told me to stick my arms in the water, up to my elbow, to gain strength to keep going. Maybe I should stick my legs in the water and walk a bit, since I use my legs to walk, not my arms? Dad said, you can put your arms in but not your legs, because you might catch a cold. The water in the pond was freezing. I drank some water out of the bottle, though I wasn't that thirsty. When I saw how much Dad drank, I was afraid he'd drink it all and not leave any for me. Want some? Yes, I said, and I drank a little, and Dad poured the rest out onto the grass. There's a spring not far from here and its water is crystal clear, we'll refill the bottle there. We left the pond and sat down on a small hill to rest and admire our village. From there we could see the two rivers, one with water and one without, the bridge and piles of trash, like tiny mountains, the sheepfold with its sheep that were standing still and resting, the big pond, the teeny tiny houses and the forest surrounding them, like a royal mantle.

— It's so beautiful! I said.

— Look at our house, look at our walnut tree. Dad pointed out the tree using a long piece of grass, an old foxtail. Though it was very far away, the walnut tree at our gate hadn't become blue, it was gray. It wasn't like the walnut trees at the horizon.

Back on the road.

— Let's see if the currants are ripe yet, but walk quickly and pick only big berries, as many as can fit in your pockets. After they're full, don't pick any more, because I'll be picking some too for you to eat on the way, and we'll pick some for Mom on the way back, so we're not caught out here when the sun is hottest. We'll cool off in a grove, in the shade, when the sun starts burning.

— What a beautiful village we have! Dad, is our village the most beautiful one in the world?

— For us, yes, but for our neighbors, their village is the most beautiful one in the world.

All of our villages are almost the same, they all have ponds, forests, sheepfolds. Our river empties out into the Răut, but before it gets there, it passes through about twenty other villages and everyone is fond of it, and each village considers it to be the village's river. And some villages even have bigger rivers, older forests, and steeper hills, like the cliffs on the coast of the sea.

The currant bushes grew in long rows that seemed endless. Dad went down one row, I went down another, and when I'd fall behind, Dad would yell, hurry up. He'd say: The currants are riper here, as if I could see them in his row. The bushes were much taller than me, but more berries were ripe at the bottom, near the ground, than up high, at the top. I found some orange berries, and some red ones, but Dad said that the black ones are best. He gave me a bit of bread to eat after the currants, because they're a bit sour and they'll make me hungry. But he didn't eat any. After the currant bushes, we reached the spring. We drank a little and filled the bottle up with water. Someone had carved the year 1978 into the stone, that's when they had paved the spring, they had made it more beautiful, but water had been flowing from it long before, it's the oldest spring in the village, water has been flowing here since the world began.

We only had one hill left. That's where our wheat is. It grew this year, we'll need money for the combine. The machinery and labor cost more than the harvest. Again I couldn't see my blue walnut trees.

— We're in a valley, that's why you can't see them. I'm going to go see about the wheat, and you, take this path, straight ahead, go and see the walnut trees. When you've climbed up, you've reached the horizon.

— I thought you didn't know.

— You thought your dad was dumb. When you get there,

say an Our Father, cross yourself three times and think about the health of your loved ones. Don't walk fast, because you'll get tired. It seems close, but it isn't. I'll wait for you in the grove. Reach the horizon, look at the walnut trees, then take the path down, straight into the grove. If you need anything, yell for me because I'll hear you. And bring back a walnut or two, let's see if they're good. I brought my pocketknife.

The horizon was right behind the walnut trees. Or rather, the walnut trees were at the edge of the path, and the path disappeared beyond the horizon.

From here, the horizon was a hilltop, like all the others I had climbed until now. I walked and walked and suddenly I was there. I closed my eyes and imagined my porch and the far-off and inaccessible edges of the hills that I had seen from there. I opened my eyes and saw the line where the earth joins with the sky. I stretched out my hand and lifted a finger over the horizon, my finger, like a mushroom without a cap. I'm here! I'm at the top of the hill, right on the line dividing heaven and earth. When you step onto the horizon, it doesn't seem like an edge anymore, I was standing in the middle of it. On the hilltop, I was in the middle of the wheat fields and my village, with everything surrounding it, it almost looked the same as the other little village on the other side of the horizon. Green forests surrounded the village there as well, and itty-bitty winding roads snuck in between houses, there were two little ponds, a river, I don't know if ours flows through that village too or if it's a different one. At the top of their hill, I saw another horizon. It was almost as far away as this one that I had been dreaming about on my porch had been. With green, yellow, and blue hills, with clear lines separating the earth and the sky. That was my discovery. I'm still too small and tired for the next horizon. I'm content with this one. I sat down on the warm dirt and looked around, I looked at the other village, I'll ask Dad what its name is, then I looked up at the sky. At home, in our yard, there's air when you look up, and here it's the sky, big, clean, without any pollution, roofs, or shady trees. It was as if I were sitting right in heaven. There was even a breeze cooling me down. Dad didn't yell for me, nor did I want him to yell for me. The walnut trees from the horizon are blue after all, from so much sky, probably. I looked at the grove where my dad was resting. At the horizon, everything belongs to you. All the land around me, the clean and peaceful sky, everything was mine. Thinking about all that wealth left me breathless. I was only seven years old, but I seemed to be the same age as Dad. I was grown-up, I was strong, I was happy. I had conquered the first horizon in my life.

My brothers don't search for the horizon from our porch. And I can't tell them that it exists. They're probably still too young. There are things you have to come to by yourself, without advice, directions, or spoon-fed answers. If you don't want to see it, if you don't search for it or dream about it, the horizon is the edge of a path and that's all.

℀

I received a phone call from Lucian. He knew that no one had told me. Grandma had died yesterday morning . . . I'm crying and I don't even know if it's because I'm mourning my grandmother or because I'm happy that Mom and Dad will finally come home.